Que

FIRE★WC

Strength Spee Courage

Luck Charm Attraction = **LP**

Starting:

Current:

Number of Successful Battles:

BATTLE SCORES

Enemy:	Enemy:
Enemy LIFE POINTS:	Enemy LIFE POINTS:
Result of Battle:	Result of Battle:
Damage done (modified by skill and weapons used):	Damage done (modified by skill and weapons used):
Enemy's final LIFE POINTS:	Enemy's final LIFE POINTS:

Enemy: Enemy LIFE POINTS: Result of Battle: Damage done (modified by skill and weapons used): Enemy's final LIFE POINTS:	Enemy: Enemy LIFE POINTS: Result of Battle: Damage done (modified by skill and weapons used): Enemy's final LIFE POINTS:
Enemy: Enemy LIFE POINTS: Result of Battle: Damage done (modified by skill and weapons used): Enemy's final LIFE POINTS:	Enemy: Enemy LIFE POINTS: Result of Battle: Damage done (modified by skill and weapons used): Enemy's final LIFE POINTS:
Enemy: Enemy LIFE POINTS: Result of Battle: Damage done (modified by skill and weapons used): Enemy's final LIFE POINTS:	Enemy: Enemy LIFE POINTS: Result of Battle: Damage done (modified by skill and weapons used): Enemy's final LIFE POINTS:

About the author

Since he was seventeen, J. H. Brennan has been interested in magic, spells and wizardry. He has written, among many other books, three volumes on magic and is working on more.

In 1983 he brought out two Fantasy Role-Play games – *Man, Myth & Magic* and TIMESHIP. Earlier in 1984, Armada published his highly successful *Grailquest*. In writing the *Demonspawn* series (which are really Fantasy Role games in book form for a single player) he has managed to combine his favourite interests.

He lives in a centuries-old thatched cottage in Ireland, surrounded by a garden full of nature sprites.

Sagas of the Demonspawn

Book One FIRE*WOLF
Book Two THE CRYPTS OF TERROR

J. H. Brennan

Fire*Wolf

SAGAS OF THE
DEMONSPAWN
BOOK 1

Fontana Paperbacks

First published in the UK in 1984
by Fontana Paperbacks,
8 Grafton Street, London W1X 3LA

Map by Ken Lewis

Made and printed in Great Britain by
William Collins Sons & Co. Ltd, Glasgow

CONTENTS

FANTASY ROLE PLAY

This is a different kind of book. Before you start to read it, you should know how and why.

Most novels you simply read and (hopefully) enjoy. *This* novel you take part in.

You may find that a pretty weird experience. You may also find it utterly addictive.

Because this book is very different from most other novels on the market, we call it a *participation* novel.

Participation novels are based on certain techniques developed in the strange world of Fantasy Role Play games.

If you have played, or are familiar with, Fantasy Role Play games, you can safely skip the next few paragraphs. If not, they will give you a little interesting background.

The world's first Fantasy Role Play game was developed comparatively recently, in the early 1970s. It was so different from all the other games around at that time that none of the big publishers wanted to buy it. So the young Americans who developed it decided to publish it themselves.

After a slow start, that game started to eat up big chunks of the game-buying market. Other game designers and publishers took notice. More Fantasy Role Play games were produced. Specialist magazines were published for Role Players. All of a sudden, Fantasy Role Play was big business.

It still is and it's still growing.

If you've never played a full-scale FRP (Fantasy Role Play) game and want to start, I might as well recommend my own FRP game systems, *Timeship* and *Man, Myth & Magic*, available in British game shops.

Most FRP games are played in a group. You're shown a simple way of creating a fictional character and you run that character, alongside characters created by other members of your group, through a specially written adventure.

To do this, you need a sort of referee called a Game Master. It's great fun, but it does take a lot of dedicated people to get the whole thing up and running.

Since not every Role Player has a group of enthusiastic friends they can call on every time they feel like it, the FRP game industry developed something called a Solo Adventure.

The name says it all. In a Solo Adventure, you don't need a Game Master or a player group. All you need is your favourite FRP system and the adventure scenario. You create your character and run that character through the adventure all on your own.

You can guess what's coming next. Why not create a Solo Adventure that is complete in itself? One that doesn't even need you to lay out hard-earned extra cash to buy a complicated Role Play system?

Why not indeed? In the present book we've done just that, using elements from literature and elements from Fantasy Role Play to create a very special reader/player experience.

GETTING STARTED

You'll need dice.

Well, you'll nee one dice anyway, although if you can lay your hands easily on two that would be better. We're talking ordinary six-sided dice here, nothing fancy.

You'll also need paper and something to write with. If you happen to own a pocket calculator, get that too. It's not in the least necessary but it could be handy.

With this equipment, you may proceed bravely to the next section.

Creating a Character

If you're not familiar with FRP, you could be surprised to learn the chances are you'll be reading this book more than once. This is because you – by which I mean your *character* in the book – will probably get killed first or second time around. Unlike the real world where it's usually a bit of a nuisance, death lends spice to an FRP adventure.

In a full-blown Fantasy Role Play game, creating your character can be a complicated and long-drawn-out process. Here it isn't, partly because we've made it simple, partly because the very nature of a participation novel means a lot of the work is done for you.

The way you create your character is this:

Take a look at the little table below.

STRENGTH
SPEED
STAMINA
COURAGE
SKILL

These are, as you can see, certain fundamental characteristics of a personality. Not *all* the characteristics of a personality, admittedly, but the major characteristics associated with the popular human occupation of fighting. Fighting is very important in an adventure, as you'll find.

To make sure your character is well rounded, we're going to add in a few more characteristics. These are:

LUCK
CHARM
ATTRACTION

This is where you get to work.

Take your pair of dice and roll them against the first heading in our table: STRENGTH. (If you couldn't find a pair of dice, roll one die twice. It amounts to the same thing; it only takes longer.)

When you've rolled the dice, multiply the result you got by 8. (Now you know why the calculator comes in handy!) Write down the result in the space opposite STRENGTH in the table. Or if you don't want to mark the book, copy out the table on a separate sheet of paper.

Now make double dice rolls against each of the other headings on the table except SKILL and in each case multiply the result by 8 before writing it down. The SKILL heading you should leave blank for the moment.

What you've got now is a series of headings with numbers written opposite them. Together, these headings and numbers represent the central skeleton of your fictional character, the selfsame character who is destined to become the hero of this book. Each figure you've written down represents the *percentage* of the particular quality your personal character now has at this particular time. Because the percentages were derived at random, you can see you've gone a long way towards creating a unique personality for your character.

If you're a mathematician and haven't become totally dazzled by this fascinating start to a novel, you will already have noticed something wrong here. We've been talking about percentages, but if you roll two six-sided dice and multiply the result by 8, the highest possible answer you can get is 96 – 4 short of 100%. Don't let this worry you. Only Allah is perfect, as the Arabs are fond of telling us. More to the point, the perfect character gets to have pretty boring adventures. So we'll continue to talk about percentages, but remember that however good they are, nobody achieves the absolute maximum.

There is one heading in your table that's left blank. It's the heading of SKILL. Don't let this worry you either. SKILL isn't something you're born with: it's something you learn. You'll pick up your SKILL figure in the course of your adventure. More about that later. At the moment you've made a healthy start by creating your character.

The next thing you need to know is how he fights.

Fighting the Foe

When the central character in your ordinary run-of-the-mill novel gets into a spot of bother, it's the author who decides whether he comes out of it in one piece. In a participation novel, by contrast, that decision is always left to you, the reader. It is your skill, judgement and luck which determine combat outcomes. (Not to mention such vital factors as who marries the princess and who only gets to kiss frogs.)

In order to achieve this sort of control over the participation novel experience, you will need to invest just a little time and effort into learning the following Rules of Combat. They may look complicated at first, but that's only because they're unfamiliar. You'll soon get the hang of them and by the time they become really important in your forthcoming adventure, you will be using them automatically. As an added bonus, learning these rules now means you can enjoy other participation novels without prior preparation – at least you can enjoy *my* other participation novels without prior preparation.

Life and Death

Whether your character lives or dies depends ultimately on how well you manage to conserve his LIFE POINTS.

To get an idea of your character's current LIFE POINTS (LP for short) all you need do is add together the numbers you filled in on your table. In other words, the formula for start-up LP is:

STRENGTH+SPEED+STAMINA+COURAGE+
LUCK+CHARM+ATTRACTION = LIFE POINTS.

In the course of the adventure as your character develops SKILL, total LP will increase as SKILL points are added on.

But don't run away with the idea that your character's LIFE POINTS are static. They aren't. You'll find they vary through the adventure. He will lose LP in fights and several other interesting situations and regain LP through rest, healing and so on. At no time, however, will the LP ever rise above the figure you started off with, except for the additions given by SKILL development.

Here's the $64,000 Rule:

If your character's LIFE POINTS *ever drop to zero (or below) he's dead.*

When that happens, you go back to the beginning and roll up another incarnation for your character.

Rules of Combat

Straight fights and other combat situations in a participation novel are decided by dice rolls, with results subject to certain modifications. The way it works is this:

1. First Strike.
Unless otherwise stated, you start by deciding who gets in the first move. This is done by rolling two dice for your character and two dice for the enemy he's facing. Add your SPEED, COURAGE and LUCK figures to the result of your character's roll. Add the enemy's SPEED, COURAGE and LUCK figures to his result. Compare the final figures. Whoever has the highest gets his move in first.

2. Beginning Combat.
Once First Strike has been decided, you and your enemy take it turn and turn about to attack one another until the combat is resolved by death, defeat, retreat or some other factor.

3. Successful Hit.
For each blow aimed in combat, roll two dice. Fundamentally, a score of 7 or better indicates that the blow has landed. Anything less than 7 counts as a miss. But this figure will always be modified by your SKILL and, to some extent, by your LUCK. For every 10 points of SKILL you acquire, you can take 1 point off the score you need to hit. If, for example, you find yourself with 20 SKILL points, then you only need a 5 to hit. But it must be 10 *full* SKILL points. Until your SKILL reaches 10, there is no SKILL modification. Even when it reaches 19, you still modify only by 1. And so on. Naturally, your enemy's ability to hit you is modified in exactly the same way. The LUCK modification is easier and you can work it out right now. If your LUCK figure stands at 72 or better, you can subtract 1 from the

score you need to hit. In other words, if your LUCK is 72 or higher, you need only throw a 6 or better to indicate your blow has been successful. And again, the same goes for your opponent.

4. Damage.
Once the dice and modifications show you've successfully defeated your opponent, the time comes to calculate the damage you may have caused him. This is easily done.

First, take note of how many points *more than* your hit figure were shown on the dice roll. (If you need, say, a modified 5 to hit because of your SKILL and LUCK and you actually roll 10, then you have rolled 5 more than your hit figure.) Multiply this figure by 10 to show the basic damage scored.

But damage too is always modified. For every 8 points of STRENGTH you have, you can add 1 point to any damage you score. Furthermore, if you hit your opponent with a weapon, you will obviously do more damage than if you simply used your fist, so various weapons also add to damage scored. You'll find an easy reference table on page 18 showing the additional damage associated with various weapons. Equally obviously, the use of armour or a shield *subtracts* from any damage caused. On the same table, you will find the figures related to various types of armour.

Once you have calculated and modified the damage, the final figure is subtracted from your enemy's current LIFE POINTS. (And the same goes for damage scored against your character.) As we said earlier, once the LP total reaches zero, death sets in.

5. Avoiding Death.
   There is only one slim chance of avoiding death should you find your LP have dropped to zero or below. This is associated with your LUCK. Should you find your character has apparently been killed, you are permitted one (only) roll of two dice, the result of which should be multiplied by 8. If the final figure is *less* than your LUCK percentage, then you may rerun the fight from the beginning, with both you and your enemy starting at your full natural LIFE POINT total. Should your enemy kill you the second time around, you do NOT have another opportunity to test your LUCK.

6. Endurance.
   How long you can continue fighting blow for blow depends on your STAMINA figure. Divide this figure by 10 (rounding down to the nearest whole number) to discover how many combat rounds you can go without a rest. Once you reach that figure during a fight, you must rest for two combat rounds to get your breath back. This means, in effect, that your enemy gets two free chances to strike at you without your being able to strike back.

Magic

It's probably as well to warn you that magic works in the fantasy world you're about to enter via your character. But that's not to say it's commonplace. You *may* meet a magician, sorcerer or witch. You *may* even stumble on some magic of your own. If you do, you'll get an explanation of how magic works at that time.

Gaining Skill

SKILL is gained only by experience. For every fight you undertake (and survive!) you may add 1 point to your SKILL total. This adds to your overall LIFE POINTS and will eventually begin to add to your chances of making a successful hit during combat.

And here's the good news. Any SKILL you pick up in this way *stays with you* if you survive your current adventure.

That means you can *begin* your next participation novel in this series with a certain amount of SKILL to your credit. It may not be a lot, but it could mean the difference between life and death.

WEAPONS/ARMOUR DAMAGE
MODIFICATION TABLE

Arrow	+10
Axe	+15
Club	+8
Dagger	+5
Flail	+7
Halbert	+12
Lance	+12
Mace	+14
Spear	+12
Sword	+10

Chain mail	−8
Leather armour	−5
Plate mail	−12
Shield	−7

An armoured fighter using a shield will benefit from both, but the value of the shield in this situation drops to −5 since the wearing of armour slows down its usage.

All figures given refer to *standard* weapons and armour only. Magical weapons and armour give additional damage and protection if you are lucky enough to find them, as you will certainly discover if the situation arises.

Playing this Book

Your efforts with the dice have given you the skeleton of a character, not the character itself.

If we were playing an FRP game, you would have to do a great deal more work before you could get started. You would have to sort through various character classes, purchase arms and armour and make all sorts of preliminary decisions which, while interesting enough first time round, become a bore thereafter.

The good news is that none of this is at all necessary in a participation novel. That work has all been done for you. What happens next is simple. Armed with your trusty dice, your paper and your pen (which in this instance is not only mightier than the sword, but actually replaces it), you need only turn the page to step into an adventure which will live in your imagination like few you have ever read.

If you have flicked through the pages in advance, you will certainly have noticed a peculiarity about much of the book. In fact, you may well have decided whole chunks of it don't make a lot of sense. This is due to the fact that a participation novel doesn't read the same way ordinary novels do. It doesn't have a sequence starting from the first page and running page by page until the end. Instead, the action *tracks*, moving from one section to another in accordance with certain choices you make and the outcome of certain situations in which you will find yourself. This sounds complicated if you have never experienced it before, but the reality is quite straightforward, so don't get upset the first time it happens: just follow the instructions and you'll be fine.

One final word. With your intelligence and lightning fast perceptions (you bought this book, didn't you?), you will have noticed we tend to talk about your character and you as if you were one and the same. Strictly speaking you're not, of course. Your character is a fictional creation, who lives and breathes (and dies) only in the vivid fantasy world we are about to generate between us. But you will find that *identification* between yourself and your character looms very large in an adventure of this type. There will be times when you can scarcely tell which of you is which.

At present, of course, you don't even know your character's name; and as you begin to read the next few pages you will be meeting several intriguing individuals. But fear not, gentle reader, the first time you meet your hero you will recognize him instantly.

By his asterisk. (*)

FIRE*WOLF
THE ADVENTURE

Fire*wolf

PROLOGUE

Towards the finish of their Vernal Rites, the astrologers began predicting a further coming of the Demonspawn.

Olric, the Knight Regent of the Realm, whose monkish warriors would pay the blood-price if the hellish swarm in fact arrived, took the oracles seriously and called Council.

Strategies were laid, the work mainly of old Mandar, the Phlogistine General, and Ben beni bar Jain, the Shaman Wizard. There was, as Olric rightly said, a little time, even granted the astrologers were accurate. There were only three short weeks in High Summer when the snow thawed in the mountain passes. Until then, the Realm was safe.

It was those same passes which preoccupied bar Jain, who was convinced the Guild of Alchemists might be persuaded to prepare a magic powder which would have the power to cause rockfalls and thus block them permanently. Mandar, with his warrior's scepticism about matters magical, bent his attention towards a second line of defence, an interesting strategic mixture of direct confrontation and ambush. It was a measure of the times that no one commented on the immorality of ambush.

Discussions on these and several less plausible alternatives ranged for days. There was little optimism abroad. The Spawn, for centuries, had done much as they pleased, even when faced by a united Realm led by a strong King. Today there was dissension in the Realm and King Voltar the Magnificent still slept his magic sleep. Olric ruled by consent of Council, insofar as anyone ruled at all. The social order survived more through habit and inertia than any real cohesion. But could it survive the Spawn?

Optimism was in short supply outside the Council too. Even the peasantry, inured to disaster by generations of hardship, grew fearful. The nobility, with far more to lose, in many instances planned flight. The Harbourmasters in the two great ports of Xanthus and Begradee found themselves abruptly rich. But for all the bribes, there were only so many sailing ships and so very many more noble families. And if one did not take to the seas, where did one go?

Despite firm pronouncements and firmer police action, the breakdown in public order was both manifest and widespread within days of the first predictions. Any other enemy might have caused concern, but scarcely panic. The Spawn, mercifully infrequent in their forays, created superstitious awe. Their resemblance to humanity was superficial. Their line descended to the Pit of Hell itself.

And then the astrologers, whose announcements had caused the panic in the first place, produced a glimmer of real hope. At the culmination of their Vernal Rites, they predicted the appearance of a new Messiah.

THE OUTCAST

Fire*Wolf was dying.

After eight days in the Wilderness, his strength was all but exhausted; his belly was no more than an aching void, his tongue large and lips parched. Legs, arms and chest were all streaked with his own blood, he could scarcely stand upright, let alone walk. Yet walk he did, in brief, staggering, swaying bursts driven by the sheer power of his Barbarian will.

He no longer knew where he was going, only that he must not stop. He could no longer count the time since the men of his rock village had driven him out for the one offence their leader could not endure. But he recalled the offence itself, his cracked lips twisting in the semblance of a ghastly smile, for Alena had been too sweet to forget. She had been sixteen years old, alive with virgin lusts and only daughter of the Chief: a potently dangerous combination and one to which Fire*Wolf had all too easily succumbed.

They had been discovered, of course. The crone who stumbled on their naked entanglement in the storage cave had hobbled away screaming, and soon afterwards the warriors had come. Even knowing their inevitable fate, Fire*Wolf and Alena had awaited them at the site of their sin. In the village there was nowhere to hide. Outside, there was nowhere to go.

Fire*Wolf might have fought when the men came, but he did not. They had their duty to the Chief and several of them were his friends. What was the point in slaughtering friends? Had he managed to dispatch a score of them (a doubtful proposition to begin with!), more would have come to take their place. A small postponement of the outcome would have made it no less inevitable.

Surprisingly, the Chief had not condemned him to the Rock, possibly in deference to Fire*Wolf's prowess as a warrior. The sentence was Exile, which amounted to death but carried less of a stigma.

So they drove him out into the Wilderness, allowing him his sword, his knife, his bow and twenty arrows, but neither water nor provisions. It was certain death in the wasteland where no game ran, where water and the edible fungus which had been his staple diet since childhood were only to be found deep underground. He might, of course, discover another of the scattered stone villages, which nurtured the tough Wilderness Barbarians like himself. But without the village Mark, he would be driven out at once, or, more likely, killed.

So, for eight days, he had wandered through the rock-wastes, his body fluids steadily leeched by the constant volcanic heat emerging from the ground beneath his feet. On the fourth day, wearily, clumsily (for he had already lost his fighting edge), he climbed a stone escarpment in the hope of discovering some rational goal; and in climbing, he fell, gouging his body on the razor sharp protrusions. Blood streamed from a dozen minor wounds and dried to give him the appearance of a monster or a walking corpse.

How much longer could Fire*Wolf endure? Fire*Wolf knew the answer even as he asked himself the question. Not much longer.

He sank wearily to his knees, bowed his head and felt the welcome comfort of a soft, grey fog descend on him. He might have embraced this fog, opened up his spirit to it as easily as his arms had opened to Alena. The fog promised him rest and freedom from pain; and Fire*Wolf knew it spoke truly. Yet the twisted knot of flint determination in his soul would not permit him to embrace the fog. With a massive effort he staggered once more to his feet. His eyes no longer saw, his ears no longer heard, his senses numbed almost beyond the reach of pain. Only his will moved him.

Then he heard the voice.

'Hold still, Fungus Feeder!'

It seemed to come from a great distance and as Fire*Wolf swung his head wearily, he could not determine the source. Nonetheless, his hand dropped to his sword. It was a man's voice and in the Wilderness, all men were enemies.

The voice giggled. 'Try to stick me, will you, Fungus Feeder? You're in no condition for a fight, that's for sure. Come on now, give yourself easement.'

Fire*Wolf felt a hand upon his arm, tried to turn to face this new danger (or the same danger, for he was not certain) and in turning stumbled, then fell not to the ground but into darkness that extended endlessly.

He awoke to coolness and returning strength, although his stomach churned and heaved as if the Minorcha Malady had seized him. He squeezed his eyes tight shut and fought down the nausea, then opened them to examine his surroundings.

He was in a cave. Not the deep caves of his stone village, for daylight streamed through the entrance only a few yards away, but a shelter which somehow cut down on the volcanic heat. A curiously musty odour assailed his nostrils, causing the gorge to rise again in his throat, but the worst of the nausea had obviously passed for he felt no real urge to vomit.

The cave was a habitation. There were skins in one corner to form a bed and roughly worked clay pots for storage and cooking. Nothing else. He was alone.

Carefully, Fire*Wolf climbed to his feet. His legs trembled and his head reeled, but for all that he felt stronger in himself than he had done for days. His mouth was less parched, the swelling of his tongue receded. He moved towards the entrance of the cave.

'You're awake now, Fungus Feeder, are you?'

It was the same voice he had heard before he finally collapsed. Again, instinctively, his hand dropped to his sword, but it was no longer there.

'Save your strength, Barbarian,' the voice said. 'I took it from you for my own protection. I grow too old for rough and tumble and while you were in no fit state to do me damage when I first set eyes on you, I could tell your strength would not desert you long.'

Fire*Wolf was staring at a slim, old man, bent over a rock crevice only twenty yards away. The gnarled hands held what appeared to be a length of twine. On the ground beside him lay Fire*Wolf's weapons.

'Who are you?' Fire*Wolf asked thickly, no longer fearing his enemy now that he had seen him, if indeed this ancient was his enemy at all.

'Me? It doesn't matter. Call me Baldar. I like the sound of that and I have forgotten my real name.'

'What are you doing?'

'Collecting water,' Baldar said, 'since you managed to deplete my small supply.'

Unthinking, Fire*Wolf said, 'There is no water at this level.'

Baldar snorted and withdrew a brimming pot from the crevice at the end of his twine. 'It is in the nature of fools to believe the whole world is like their own back yard. This is not your Deep Wilderness, Fungus Feeder. Your sturdy legs carried you far before Nature overcame them. Here on the perimeter a man may find surface water if he knows where to look.'

With no sign of frailty despite his advanced years, Baldar carried the pot back to the cave mouth. As he reached Fire*Wolf, he placed one hand squarely on his chest to encourage him to return inside. Fire*Wolf did not resist, his reluctance overcome by a mounting curiosity. Inside, he accepted the proffered pot and

Fire*Wolf and Baldar

drank deeply. The water was warm, but good. He returned the pot and waited.

'I'm right, am I not?' old Baldar asked. 'You come from the caverns of the Deep Wilderness?'

Fire*Wolf nodded.

'Thought you had, though you don't have the look of the fungus feeders. Too big. And the colouring's wrong.'

'I was not native born to the Wilderness,' Fire*Wolf said. 'I came to the stone village as a young boy. That much they told me, but how, or why or where I came from they would not tell.'

'If they know,' Baldar said. 'The Barbarians are an ignorant lot.'

Fire*Wolf held his temper in leash. The old man had helped him after all: and might be persuaded to help him further. Baldar seemed to catch the effort for he grinned slyly.

'There's another point of difference – a real Barbarian would have tried to kill me for the insult. You showed self-control. Or perhaps the gruel I fed you is still sticking in your stomach. But you'd better get used to real food, lad. You'll find no fungus here, or anywhere else in Harn.'

'Harn?' Fire*Wolf echoed.

'Aye, Harn – the name of this godforsaken land. Harn with its Reeflak Mountains and its Realm of Voltar the Magnificent, its Desert and its Wilderness, its eastern seaboard by the Tranquil Sea and its follies. Too many follies, but these may end soon if the rumours are true.' The old man glanced at him shrewdly. 'Well, Barbarian and Fungus Eater, do you have a name?'

'I am called Fire*Wolf,' Fire*Wolf said, enunciating the central guttural in the manner of the Wilderness tribes.

'As good as any,' Baldar said. 'And better than some. I take it you'll not be returning home?'

Fire*Wolf shook his head. The caverns he had long called home were no longer open to him.

'Well, where shall you be going?'

Fire*Wolf stared at him, wondering how to answer. It was a reasonable question, but one which he had not even momentarily considered. His whole attention had been concentrated on survival. But having survived, where in this strange country, this Harn, did an exiled Barbarian go? Eventually he said, 'I do not know.'

'Perhaps you'll know tomorrow,' Baldar said. 'When you're stronger still. You'd better sleep now.'

While Fire*Wolf meant to protest, he found he was indeed exhausted, so that he lay on the floor of the cave and swiftly fell into a dreamless sleep.

The following day they talked a great deal more. Baldar, it transpired, was a hermit, and had been for more than thirty years. He lived off what little the land had to offer, supplemented by the occasional offering from fools who imagined him a holy man. He claimed to loathe company, although he accepted Fire*Wolf's freely enough. On the day following Baldar actually began to teach Fire*Wolf the tricks of survival in this barren steppe on the edge of the Wilderness.

The twin suns rose and set, day after day, and Fire*Wolf totally regained his former stamina and strength. He had long since retrieved his weapons and now took to practising with them to regain his former skills.

Watching him one day, Baldar remarked: 'You are good enough to become a mercenary, Fire*Wolf, although not so good as to stay a live mercenary for long.'

Fire*Wolf grinned. He had now grown to like the old man, but thought this foolish. Baldar caught the expression and stood up. 'Let me show you then, ignorant Barbarian,' he said peevishly. 'There are two staves in the back of the cave. Bring them to me and we will have a contest. You are lucky I own no sword, otherwise your lesson might have proved lethal.'

Humouring him, Fire*Wolf fetched the staves. He was smiling as Baldar took one and dropped into a fighting stance. Then he roared with pain and fury as the old man's staff lashed out with unexpected speed to catch him a fearful crack across the ankle bone, bringing tears to his eyes and half crippling his movements.

'By the gods!' roared Fire*Wolf. 'Old man or not, you'll pay for that!'

And suddenly, there on the edges of the Wilderness, the fight was on.

*You are Fire*Wolf. Young, strong, handsome and barbaric. A man of lusts and tempers, arrogant in your certainties.*

This old man, this Baldar, has challenged you and that is enough. You bear him no ill-will despite the crack on your ankle, but all the same he must be taught a lesson. That is the Wilderness Way, your Way.

*But will the lesson be quite so easy as you imagine, Fire*Wolf? On page 248 you will find Baldar's stats (*SPEED, STRENGTH *etc.) which will help you calculate the outcome of this small battle. They are perhaps higher than you thought. Your first lesson: in Harn, things are not always as they seem.*

This will not, of course, be a fight to the death. When LIFE POINTS *on either side are reduced to 50 or below, surrender will be automatic. Even a freak blow which reduces* LIFE POINTS *to zero will not cause death here.*

*Calculate your outcome, Fire*Wolf. If you win the battle, go to* **140**. *If not, turn to* **20**.

1

For the briefest instant, Baldar stared across the cave at Fire*Wolf, stunned. Then, despite his age and apparent exhaustion, he launched himself fiercely from the straw. 'Vermin!' he screamed, as he fell again upon the big Barbarian, arms flailing wildly.

Although squatting on his haunches in the Wilderness Way and totally surprised by the ferocity of the attack, Fire*Wolf recovered quickly. Rolling away nimbly from the old man, he sprang to his feet. 'Hold hard, Baldar,' he called. 'I have no wish to injure you. It is only that I claim the right to make my own way in the world.'

But Baldar was beyond reason. 'Scum!' he shrieked, relaunching himself on the attack.

Fire*Wolf sidestepped, grinning slightly. He did not trouble to draw his sword, for the old hermit was unarmed. Nor was he unduly worried by the show of rage. In the stone village rage and frustration were commonplace.

Baldar tripped, half fell, then recovered and lashed out again. His fist caught Fire*Wolf a glancing blow. He kicked hard at the Barbarian's shins, but missed completely. Fire*Wolf reached out, seeking to catch the flailing arms and pin them. Old though he was, Baldar moved fast, twisting like an eel. Fire*Wolf felt a pinprick at his shoulder and noticed for the first time that the old hermit was clutching a sliver of sharpened bone, a weapon of desperation, seized in the heat of the moment and fortunately too small to do much damage.

'Enough, Old Man!' Fire*Wolf exclaimed again. But there was no stopping Baldar, who attacked again like a demon.

This time, however, Fire*Wolf was ready. As the old hermit closed with him, he flung his arms wide, then closed them in a fierce embrace. Baldar wriggled, struggled, but was pinned. Easily, Fire*Wolf lifted him off his feet, taking some care at least not to hurt him unduly. 'Calm yourself, Hermit,' he said sternly. 'You are too old for two fights in one day.'

Surprisingly, Baldar did calm. His muscles relaxed so that he hung limp in Fire*Wolf's arms, but his eyes remained filled with anger.

'I shall release you if you promise to behave,' Fire*Wolf told him. 'I wish only the freedom to choose my own course. I shall leave here at once since my presence disturbs you. Will you promise?'

Baldar remained dumb. His eyes turned to Fire*Wolf's shoulder.

Oddly, the pinprick from the sliver of bone was stinging fiercely now. Fire*Wolf ignored it, tightening his grip a little so that Baldar gasped. 'Come now, Old Man, your promise!'

A sly look replaced the rage in Baldar's eyes. 'You have it, Fungus Feeder, provided you leave me at once.'

'You already have my word on that,' said Fire*Wolf, releasing him. Baldar backed away, eyeing him warily.

Fire*Wolf's shoulder had begun to throb. Nonetheless, alert for another attack, he picked up his few belongings and made for the mouth of the cave.

'Farewell, Old Man,' he called back. 'I thank you for helping me when I needed it and regret I cannot help you in my turn.' Half-consciously he placed a hand on his throbbing shoulder, suspecting an infection and wondering at the speed of its development. He stepped forward and found his head was swimming. He paused, feeling a growing weakness in his legs. He swayed.

From behind him, distantly, came Baldar's voice. 'Farewell, ungrateful wretch!' It seemed to Fire*Wolf that he spat upon the cave floor. Fire*Wolf half turned, with spots of darkness dancing before his eyes. His shoulder was on fire now, the bones within his legs and arms dissolving.

'The poison is fast acting,' Baldar remarked. 'You will feel less pain than you deserve.'

2

The dancing spots before Fire*Wolf's eyes coalesced into a single well of darkness as he pitched forward blindly.

An unworthy fate for heroes, but one written in the Book of Fate for those who commit the sin of ingratitude. Go to **13**.

2

The creature was one Fire*Wolf had not seen before, although the heavy mane, feline features and striped pelt suggested it might be the tigon, often mentioned by the Keeper of Histories in the stone village.

At first, he caught sight of it only briefly, a tawny shape in the undergrowth, moving with silent ease. But it was stalking him, and in time grew bolder so that, within an hour, he saw the beast clearly, fang and claw.

For a time he thought he could elude it, but the tigon was both cunning and determined. Eventually Fire*Wolf was determined to make a stand, since there seemed no question of outrunning his pursuer. Consequently he chose a mound of high ground, comparatively free of vegetation so that the beast would have no cover when it made its final charge. He drew his sword and lay down beside it on the ground, pretending sleep: a tempting target for a hungry hunter.

Fire*Wolf waited.

The tigon was cautious. Through slitted eyes Fire*Wolf watched it circle him again and again, breaking cover only briefly, sniffing the air nervously.

Then, with no warning at all, it charged.

Fire*Wolf and the tigon

And Fire*Wolf, sword in hand, rose to meet it.

*Turn to page 248 for tigon combat stats, then calculate the outcome of the fight. If Fire*Wolf dies beneath the rending claws, turn to* **13**. *Should our hero defeat the tigon, turn to* **5**.

3

At first it was no more than a prickling sensation on the nape of the neck. But Fire*Wolf had learned to trust his instincts and stopped his steady trot to glance around, senses straining.

He saw nothing, but at the instant of his stopping thought he heard a sound. He froze, listening intently. Wind sighed through the grass beneath his feet. He half turned, reaching for his sword.

And then the constrictor lizard was upon him.

*Poor Fire*Wolf. The constrictor lizard is one of the less pleasant denizens of the wilder reaches of Harn. It is a creature similar to a snake, up to eighteen feet long, and scaled. For combat stats see page 248. Calculate the outcome of the fight, allowing the constrictor first strike, for Fire*Wolf was undoubtedly surprised. If the lizard kills him, go to* **13**. *If Fire*Wolf wins, go to* **5**.

4

With no warning whatsoever, a feathered arrow embedded itself in the ground at Fire*Wolf's feet.

The Wilderness Barbarian's reaction was instantaneous. Dropping and rolling, he drew his broadsword on the instant. As he rose, he crouched to his feet again. Two men broke cover from the shrub no more than fifteen feet away from him. Both were burly fellows, roughly dressed in the drab green homespun that marked the Bandit Guild of Harn. One carried a sword, the other a bow which he was even now exchanging for his own sword. Both were grinning.

'Fast reactions, Traveller!' called the foremost of the bandits cheerfully. 'But now you may put away your weapon. We require only your belongings, not your life!'

Still crouched, Fire*Wolf watched them walk towards him, swords held casually relaxed, a touch of swagger in their step. It was that swagger which gave him confidence. These men were too sure of themselves by half, accustomed to dealing with merchants and friars who offered gold in place of resistance. But their present prey was of a different mettle. Their present opponent was a Wilderness Barbarian.

'What is it you require of me?' he asked softly, maintaining his stance.

'Why, no more than what you have, Traveller. A small donation for safe passage: a coin or two . . .' He held out one broad hand, still grinning.

And with a swift movement of his sword, Fire*Wolf severed it completely from his arm.

*An unfriendly gesture, but the Wilderness Way. Now Fire*Wolf must fight both villains and defeat them. For bandit combat stats, turn to page 248 and calculate the outcome. (The bandit with the severed hand begins the fight with 20* LIFE POINTS *subtracted from his total and will automatically lose 10* *more in each combat round additional to any further damage Fire*Wolf may occasion him.) Should the bandits kill Fire*Wolf, as they will assuredly attempt to do, go to* **13**. *If Fire*Wolf succeeds in killing them, go to* **5**.

5

*(Add one point to Fire*Wolf's* SKILL *for each opponent killed.)*

The encounter was a salutary lesson for Fire*Wolf for though he survived, he did not survive unscathed. His chest and abdomen were both cut and slashed quite badly. He felt weak from loss of blood. Worst of all, there was a sharp pain in his lungs when he walked, suggesting the real possibility of a cracked rib. But the Wilderness-bred body was tough and Fire*Wolf was nothing if not stoical, so he rested a little then pressed on slowly. He was, he knew, still some considerable distance from Belgardium.

The morning of the fifth day found his mind clearer after a fitful night's sleep, but his body weak. Although the weather was warm, he found himself shivering a little as he pushed himself painfully to his feet and wondered if his wounds might have become infected. By mid-morning with the sun high, he knew he was running a fever. He felt alternately hot and chill. Even small exertions exhausted him. Nonetheless, he pushed his reluctant body forward.

By evening he had travelled only a few miles and knew, with growing certainty, that unless he found help there was a very real possibility that the fight he had so recently won might yet prove his greatest defeat.

5

The grassland he was crossing gradually gave way to rougher ground so that he had to rest more and more frequently. Although he had not eaten that day, he could not hunt and even the prospect of rooting for grubs or maggots seemed beyond his immediate capabilities. His mind, so clear in the morning time, grew confused so that he began to lose his sense of direction. Eventually even his sense of purpose narrowed. He no longer searched for the mental landmarks which pointed his route to Belgardium. Instead his whole mind concentrated on the more immediate difficulties of placing one foot before the other.

Towards sunset, he topped a ridge and found himself looking out across a river valley. With no set purpose in mind, he began to stumble downwards. In his befuddled state, he did not even see the assailant who struck the blow which rendered him unconscious.

*Fire*Wolf lies in darkness, visionary fragments flitting in a slow kaleidoscope through his fevered mind. A woman's face, sad but beautiful . . . an army fighting flying demons . . . the figure of a childhood friend from the stone village. Darkness.*
Go to **6**.

THE SLAVE

6

'Easy now, Big Fellow,' a gruff, but not unkindly voice murmured in Fire*Wolf's ear.

There was a foul taste in his mouth, his head ached as if it had been split through the centre with an axe. Worse still, the world seemed to be in motion like a ship at sea. He became aware of a dull ache in his thighs and backside.

Fire*Wolf opened his eyes, shook his head painfully to clear away the mental fog.

'Easy now,' the gruff voice said again.

He was astride a horse, hands bound behind his back, ankles roped together with a bond which passed beneath the belly of the animal. Two powerful arms flanked him, holding the reins; and a hard, muscular body pressed into his back. He could hear the clink of harness, smell the sweat of beasts and men. He turned his head slightly to discover he was part of a caravan of mounts, wagons, heavily black-bearded and black-cloaked horsemen, and walking men, women and children.

Fire*Wolf half turned to catch a glimpse of the black-bearded figure on the mount behind him.

'Steady,' said the man.

'Where am I?' Fire*Wolf asked. 'Who are you?'

'Me?' came the gruff voice. I'm Tojar. Do you have a name you can remember?'

'Fire*Wolf,' Fire*Wolf muttered. He allowed himself to slump forward in the saddle and slurred his voice as if still only semi-conscious, but already his mind was racing as he attempted to identify his situation. One thing was immediately clear. He was a prisoner.

'That's a Wilderness name by the sound of it. You from the Wilderness then?'

Fire*Wolf grunted.

'Don't find many from the Wilderness in these reaches,' Tojar remarked. 'But you have the accent, that's for sure, even if you don't have the typical look.' To someone further down the line he called, 'You were right, Baj. We've got us a Wilderness Barbarian here.'

'He'll fetch a good price in Xanthus if we can keep him alive,' Baj called back. 'Especially now they're expecting trouble. His race has a reputation for breeding fighters.'

Head bowed, Fire*Wolf took in the conversation word for word. The 'good price' comment told him all he needed to know. Weakly, he asked again, 'Where are we?'

'On the trail to Xanthus,' Tojar told him. 'Know where that is?'

'No,' Fire*Wolf admitted. Not that it mattered, since he had no intention of ever arriving there. Not ever and certainly not as a slave.

Fire*Wolf and Baj

'Second largest city in Harn next to the capital,' Tojar said. 'Largest port and largest market. You'll find it a bit different from the caves you're used to.'

Fire*Wolf did not doubt it. Aloud, he asked, 'How long before we get there?'

'Two weeks' march. Time enough for you to get your strength back.'

In fact, despite the aching head and stiffness in his hands and fingers where the tight bindings had cut off the blood supply, he felt far stronger than he had done before his capture. The foul taste in his mouth, bitter and pungent, suggested he had been given some herbal healing brew. If so, it seemed to have done sterling work. He was far from fully recovered, but the intermittent fever seemed to have abated and the weakness in his legs was far less pronounced.

All the same, he allowed himself to slump still further and lapsed into silence. Whatever the reality, it was important his captors did not realize the truth of his condition. They would be far less watchful if they thought him weak and ill.

The caravan travelled for several hours without incident, then, at sunset, halted to pitch camp for the night. Tojar released the bindings from Fire*Wolf's ankles and led him to a communal yurt pitched for those who had been travelling on foot. They were a motley collection, mainly women and children with only a few dispirited men. None cared to speak to him and few even bothered to meet his eye. The fact that guards were posted round the yurt told Fire*Wolf that these were his fellow slaves.

6

As the yurt flap closed, he began to twist the bonds around his wrists.

'Don't do that,' one of the older women cautioned. 'They flog you if you untie yourself without permission.' She herself was not bound. He noticed that, in fact, few were. The ropes had been reserved for the larger, more dangerous-looking captives like himself.

'Thank you,' Fire*Wolf murmured. He sought out a space in the large tent and lay down to rest and think. Those around him seemed placid, inured to their fate, but that was their choice. Fire*Wolf himself had no plans to languish with this slaver caravan until it reached the port of Xanthus. At the same time, he needed to lay his escape plans carefully. Stronger though he was, he was not yet fully recovered. Tojar and the other black-bearded slavers were relaxed enough, obviously anticipating little trouble. All the same, they were professionals in their trade and as such would always be on the alert and know how to deal with those attempting to escape. To be successful, timing would be all important.

But how much time did he have? Two weeks to reach Xanthus, but would the slavers remain relaxed as they were now? He might have to choose between taking action now, before he reached full strength, or waiting to recover fully and run the risk that when the time came, security precautions might be far more stringent.

His thoughts were interrupted by the sudden entrance into the yurt of the man, Baj. Like all the slavers, he was dark-eyed and black-bearded, wearing the black cloak over clothing of warm, dark homespun. He looked a powerful man, broad-shouldered and muscular, although smaller in height than Fire*Wolf. He stood silhouetted in the entrance for a moment, staring arrogantly around the prisoners. Something about his gait or carriage suggested he might be just a little drunk.

'You there!' Baj called. He walked forward into the packed mass of slaves, unmindful of attack, as if he knew their spirit to be truly broken. 'You there!' he said again. 'You'll join me tonight!' He was standing before a young girl, scarcely more than sixteen or seventeen years old, with the fair hair and complexion of Northern Harn. She shrank away, eyes wide, as he reached for her.

'No!'

The cry came from an older woman, who pushed between Baj and the girl. But the burly man swept her aside easily with one rough movement of his arm. 'Come on, my pretty,' he said to the young girl. 'A man needs a little relaxation on a journey like this.'

The girl screamed as he gripped her arm and began to drag her towards the entrance of the yurt. No one moved to stop him: this was obviously a regular occurrence.

In the corner of the yurt, Fire*Wolf tucked his feet beneath him and rose, hands still bound, in a single, fluid movement.

*You are Fire*Wolf. Barbarian fire is rising in your veins at the treatment of this young girl. Your instincts insist you must attack this man: yet your* *hands remain bound, you have no weapons and your body still has not fully recovered from your last combat. What will you do, Fire*Wolf? If you follow your instincts and attack, go to* **12**. *If you decide to let events take their course without interference, go to* **8**.

7

'Out! Out!' the slaver guard called from the mouth of the yurt, the morning sun streaming in behind him. Fire*Wolf rose with the rest and filed out placidly. He had reached a decision in the night. Nothing was to be gained by direct confrontation. The best plan must be to lull these slavers into a sense of false security, persuade them that he was beaten and resigned, then strike when they least expected it.

It was a plan that called for patience, but patience was the Wilderness Way.

For two more days, Fire*Wolf grew increasingly placid and subdued, obeying orders quickly, making no overtly aggressive gesture. But all the time he remained watchful, awaiting his opportunity.

It arose on the morning of the third day, in an environment similar to that in which he had been captured. The caravan was approaching a river valley but here the entrance to the valley was narrow, steep and perilous, forcing the slavers to ride in single file.

They were obviously well accustomed to this part of their journey, for, without a word being spoken, the guards separated into two groups, one taking the vanguard, the other the rear, with the prisoners strung out between them. The narrow track was rocky and strewn with rubble, so that the horses had to pick their way carefully, slowly. To the right loomed the valley wall. To the left, a steep decline, strewn with boulders, dropping down to the valley itself.

From this high vantage point, it was possible to see a great distance. What Fire*Wolf saw interested him greatly. The main feature of the valley was a broad, slow river, flanked on one side by forest, on the other by swamp. Portions were enshrouded by heavy mists and twice he thought he caught a glimpse of a grey stone building, a fortress, keep or castle – he could not be sure which. Thick undergrowth carpeted the valley floor at the bottom of the hill, blending eventually into the heavy, sodden vegetation of the swamps. It all meant one thing. If a man could make his escape here with even a few moments' headway, the chances of his recapture would be slim indeed.

Fire*Wolf was unbound. His placid mien and patient obedience had done their work. No slaver expected trouble from this Barbarian now despite his size. But a scheme was already formulating in his mind.

He was at full strength now, his earlier injuries no more than old scar tissue on his massive frame. All the same, no one would have suspected it, for he had taken great care to move slowly, painfully over the past days. It had been only a ruse to keep his captors off their guard but now he put it to good account. As the caravan progressed at a crawl to within a few hundred feet of the valley floor, Fire*Wolf chose his spot. He clutched his abdomen and screamed, then pitched forward close to the track edge, writhing as if seized by cramps. Then, abruptly, he turned on to his back, allowing his eyes to open wide and glaze. He held his body rigid and waited.

The gods favoured Fire*Wolf that day, for it was Baj who came to investigate the trouble. So well had Fire*Wolf succeeded in assuming the demeanour of the dejected slave that Baj did not even trouble to draw a precautionary weapon as he bent to examine the prostrate Barbarian.

As he stooped, Fire*Wolf took him by the throat.

*Brave Fire*Wolf, an unforgiving man in the Barbarian Way. But cunning too, for it will take some time before the remaining guards can negotiate the narrow path to come to the aid of their companion. The fight is one to one here. Check Baj's combat stats on page 248 and calculate the outcome. Baj will not be able to use a weapon. It is a fight with bare hands, to the death. If Baj wins, go to* **13**. *If Fire*Wolf succeeds in strangling the slaver, go to* **11**.

8

The girl twisted, attempting to bite Baj's hand – a movement which earned her a sharp cuff on the side of the head so that she gasped and staggered as he dragged her from the yurt. In the silence that followed, the prisoners could hear her screams dying away in the distance.

Fire*Wolf slowly returned to his space and squatted in the Wilderness Way. He had been powerless to act and the feeling of helplessness was gall to his mouth. But the incident had, at least, resolved his dilemma. There was no longer any question of awaiting his opportunity. He must escape now, at the earliest possible moment. Now he was determined that when he left this place, he would take the life of Baj with him. Somehow the man would pay for the brutal act he was even now committing.

Quietly, in the semi-darkness of the yurt, Fire*Wolf began to work again at the bonds around his wrists.

Go now to 7.

9

*(Add one point to Fire*Wolf's* SKILL.*)*

They dragged him to the outskirts of the encampment, where any screams he might make would disturb no one, and flogged him.

The punishment was administered without rancour, but with a dreadful efficiency which peeled the skin from his back and caused a flood of pain which, though it failed to make him scream, sent his senses reeling. Then, when it was over, he was carried back to the slave yurt barely conscious. They dropped him unceremoniously in a heap beside the flap and left without a backwards glance. This was, it seemed, routine for the slavers, an efficient means of ensuring troublemakers learned to make no trouble in the future. No wonder the other prisoners were subdued.

Fire*Wolf could not say how long he lay there, teetering on the edge of blackness, before he felt a gentle hand upon his arm, heard a quiet voice beside his ear.

'Are you alive, Barbarian?'

'Alive?' whispered Fire*Wolf hoarsely. 'Alive, aye, if only barely.' He turned painfully to find himself looking into the face of the older woman who had tried to save the girl. Behind her he could just make out the shadowy form of the girl herself.

'I am Jaen,' the woman said, 'mother of Jara, the girl you saved.'

Fire*Wolf grunted.

'Baj is a pig,' Jaen said. 'They all are, these slavers. I wished to thank you, and to express my sorrow at the pain your actions have brought you.'

Fire*Wolf shrugged, a movement which sent jagged spikes of pain through his bleeding back. 'My actions are my own responsibility,' he said.

'Your actions were on my daughter's behalf. For that I thank you and beg you to accept this gift.' With which she pressed a small pouch into Fire*Wolf's hand, unbound now since the flogging.

'There is no need . . .' Fire*Wolf began. But his words came too late, for Jaen had faded into the darkness of the yurt.

Fire*Wolf turned on his side and tried to compose himself for sleep, sinking deep into that central stillness which shielded him from pain. But despite his Barbarian resilience, he slept fitfully, and in the night was fully awakened by a presence beside him in the darkness, a small, gentle hand which caressed him.

'Here, Barbarian,' a girl's voice whispered. 'Have that comfort which I denied the slaver.'

9

While Fire*Wolf was convinced that, in his pain and his exhaustion, he was in no state whatsoever to take that which was offered, time and the patient ministrations of those gentle hands proved Fire*Wolf wrong.

He awoke at dawn to the sound of shouted orders from the slavers as they prepared to break camp. He was alone now where he lay, but the small leather pouch Jaen had given him lay on the ground beside him. He glanced inside and found a single, highly polished, rounded stone, jet black, veined with emerald green and quite unlike anything he had ever seen. It was not a gemstone, not even one of the many semi-precious stones which served as ornamentation for the poorer classes. But as he handled it, a curious feeling of well-being stole through his aching frame. In a moment the sensation peaked, then receded, leaving him stronger than before, with less stiffness in his muscles, less pain in his back.

Thoughtfully, he placed the stone back in its leather pouch and hid it in his loincloth where the guards were unlikely to find it.

*Fortune sometimes favours the brave, it seems. For gallant Fire*Wolf is now the owner of a sorcerous artifact, a healing stone which will, between rounds of combat, permit him to regain a single die roll of lost* LIFE POINTS. *The Healing Stone contains 50* LIFE POINTS *in all, but will recharge itself in 48 hours after combat is over. The stone may only be used to regain lost* LIFE POINTS *not to generate excess. Go now to* **7**.

10

Thus, Fire*Wolf the Wilderness Barbarian, already exiled from the only home he ever knew, left the rude cave of Baldar the Hermit on a mission which was to carry him to broader horizons than he ever suspected existed.

He carried with him his sword, his bow and twenty arrows, a filled waterskin to see him safely through what remained of the Wilderness, some dried provisions (although Baldar assured him that hunting-gathering would soon be possible) and two additional small gifts from Baldar. The first of these was a purse containing ten of the small golden coins which were, so Baldar assured him, the common currency of Harn, and a slim-bladed dagger, poison-tipped, lest anyone attempted to steal his gold. He had accepted the dagger with reluctance, at Baldar's insistence. He disliked the idea of poison, for such weapons went contrary to all he had been taught to believe in the Wilderness. But he took it to please the old man and promised himself it would never be used, except in direst emergency.

In his head, Fire*Wolf carried instructions. Baldar had offered to draw him a map on cloth, but Fire*Wolf was unfamiliar with such things and preferred the Wilderness Way of memory. As Baldar described the landmarks, Fire*Wolf pictured them in his mind, linking each, with each and had only to conjure the same vision as he walked in order to find his place.

For a day and a night the going remained rough, but gradually, as Baldar had promised, the Wilderness edge gave way to shrub, then grassland increasingly fertile. He saw game and eventually, as his small stock of provisions ran out, was forced to hunt. He proved skilful enough: all children of the Wilderness, male and female, were taught archery from childhood on account of the frequent wars between the various stone villages, and animals were easier prey than people for at least they did not shoot back. His main concern was eating meat, which revolted him even when cooked as Baldar had shown him. A lifelong diet of fungus had conditioned his palate so that even vegetables seemed repulsive. But in the Wilderness Way he was a realist. If there was no fungus, then meat and vegetables it would have to be. He did, however, supplement his diet with a worthy supply of maggots and grubs – delicacies far more plentiful here than anywhere in the Wilderness.

For almost four days, Fire*Wolf travelled without encountering a soul. Then, on the afternoon of the fourth day. . .

*The ways of Fate are strange, Fire*Wolf. Roll one (only) die. Compare the result with the table below, then turn to the section indicated.*

Score	*Section*
1 or 2 go to	**2**
3 or 4 go to	**3**
5 or 6 go to	**4**

11

The instant Baj went limp, Fire*Wolf jerked away from the corpse. He leapt to the edge of the track and jumped to slide, stumble and roll down the steep decline into the valley. Behind him he could hear the excited shouts of the slavers – and not a little encouragement from his fellow slaves.

He had hoped his surprise move might have given him a few moments, headstart. The decline was too steep for the horses so he knew that the slavers would have to follow him on foot. But in the event, he reached the bottom, cut and bruised, with no pursuit at all. One of the black cloaks loosed a desultory arrow, which flew far wide of its mark, but the remainder neither fired nor attempted to follow.

Fire*Wolf plunged into the cover of the undergrowth, then paused to watch. To his amazement, there was still no pursuit. Those slavers who had dismounted in the excitement now climbed back into their saddles and in a moment, the caravan was moving on as if nothing had happened. He noticed now for the first time that the track it was following did not lead down into the valley itself, but rather skirted the edge before rising again, then twisting so that the mounted figures and their walking captives were soon completely out of sight.

The development disturbed Fire*Wolf far more than the pursuit he had expected. To the slavers he was valuable property. Only a day before he had heard Tojar discussing the prices of fighting slaves at Xanthus. They had always been high, apparently, and now, with some sort of national emergency declared, they had doubled overnight. Yet for Fire*Wolf, escape had been simplicity itself. His plunge to the valley floor had cost him no more than a few scratches and bruises. By abandoning their horses even the least athletic of the slavers could have followed easily. But none had, even though he had killed one of their number. Why?

Fire*Wolf waited, immobile as a hunted animal. For almost an hour he scarcely moved a muscle, all the time suspecting the possibility of a trap. But the slavers did not return, nor was there any indication of their approach from another direction. They had abandoned him. Why?

But puzzled though he was, Fire*Wolf remained a man of action rather than a philosopher. If they had abandoned him, they had abandoned him and the Wilderness gods were to be thanked for that. He rose, stretching to ease the cramps and aches immobility had brought to his muscles, then set out with a cheerful heart to place as much distance as he could between the caravan and himself.

Fire*Wolf moved deeper into the valley.

*The Annals of Harn may yet describe him as Fire*Wolf the Thoughtless, for if the slavers failed to follow, would it not suggest that their knowledge of something in the valley itself caused them to pause? Nonetheless, Fire*Wolf is committed now. Turn to* **14** *to follow his adventures in the valley.*

12

With an animal growl deep in his throat, Fire*Wolf launched himself across the yurt in a flying dropkick that connected heavily and violently with Baj's back. The slaver released the girl, stumbled and fell heavily. Fire*Wolf, hands still bound, rolled nimbly to his feet and kicked again, viciously, as Baj shook himself and began to climb upright. The second kick took the slaver in the throat, spinning him almost totally around, but he was tough and recovered quickly.

Baj backed away warily and drew his sword. 'Guards!' he called hoarsely. 'To me!'

Fire*Wolf remained immobile. Angry or not, he knew better than to tackle a sword with bare hands – and those hands tied. In such circumstances, patience was the Wilderness Way.

The yurt filled with more than a dozen guards, black-bearded and black-cloaked twins of Baj himself.

'The Barbarian attacked me,' Baj explained. With his comrades present, he relaxed his guard and dropped his sword point. 'We'd better . . .'

At once, Fire*Wolf acted. A third kick, carrying the full force of his whole body, caught Baj directly in the groin so that he bent double, retched, vomited, then tumbled, eyes glazed, to the ground.

Fire*Wolf made no movement to resist as the guards seized him and dragged him roughly from the tent. There was no doubt in his mind that the slavers would punish him – perhaps even kill him – for his attack on their colleague. But for the moment his Barbarian soul was content. Baj would be in no condition to pleasure himself with any reluctant woman that night, or for many nights to come.

*Is it death for Fire*Wolf following his rash attack? Follow him now to* **9** *where his immediate fate awaits him.*

13

Thus died the hero Fire*Wolf.

Or perhaps the word 'died' is inaccurate, for the universe – Fire*Wolf's universe – is a mysterious place, full of strange possibilities.

13

One such possibility is reincarnation.

Any reader finding himself or herself at this section may take the opportunity to create a new (and hopefully better) Fire*Wolf by returning to the introductory pages of this book and rolling up new characteristics for him.

Once recreated, Fire*Wolf may be reborn at the beginning of his great adventure, lacking SKILL but not the knowledge he has gained. This knowledge will obviously allow him to retrace his steps quickly, avoiding past mistakes, exploring possibilities he ignored on his former journeying.

Thus died Fire*Wolf.

But his death was a new beginning.

THE FUGITIVE

14

Fire*Wolf grew chill. The sun was still warm overhead, but a pall of mist rising from the swamplands sucked the warmth from his bones.

Fire*Wolf grew fearful. He was beginning slowly to realize why the slavers had not followed him into this valley. An eldritch gloom clung to the swamplands near the river. There was too little sound. In any land like this, there should have been a thousand noises: insects, small animals and birds. Here there was none. Silence brooded in the green and dismal gloom.

Swift movement was impossible. Here, in the swamp, the soft ground sucked at his feet, the tangled vegetation gripped his legs and arms, making every stride an effort. He was, so far as he could judge, moving parallel to the river in the approximate direction of the great stone building he had spotted briefly from the valley wall.

He could not say how he first knew something was following him. His nostrils caught no scent, his ears no sound. But his whole instinct, finely honed by years in the Wilderness, told him there was something: and that something getting closer. His mind created pictures of a creature unlike any he had ever known, a beast of cunning and ferocity. He shook his head to try to clear away the vision, but it remained stubbornly.

Fire*Wolf changed direction.

For just the barest instant he thought he might have eluded his pursuer, but then his instincts told him it was following again. It was now closer if anything. He could still hear nothing, see nothing, scent nothing, yet his mind was setting up a clamour close to panic. He had no doubt at all he had become prey to some predator and the creature was closing for the kill.

Fire*Wolf stopped. He was without a weapon of any sort. While the Wilderness Way had taught him many tricks of unarmed combat and survival, he knew that in his present situation he would not last more than minutes against any of the larger beasts of Harn. He looked around and at last found a hefty, broken bough, slick with swamp slime but at least unrotted. He wiped away the slime as best he could and hefted the bough in his strong right hand. A club had never been his favourite weapon, but it was all he had.

Fire*Wolf waited. In time the creature came for him.

It was immense. A swamp reptile of some unknown species, some fifteen feet long from tip of snout to tip of tail and standing almost eight feet tall at the shoulder. The muscular body was armoured with glistening green scales so that it blended with its background almost to perfection. Half-open jaws revealed fangs four inches long. The shortened forelegs ended in vicious, slime-tipped claws. The great head swung slowly side to side, searching. A white, nictating membrane flicked spasmodically across the eyes.

THE FUGITIVE

14

Fire*Wolf grew chill. The sun was still warm overhead, but a pall of mist rising from the swamplands sucked the warmth from his bones.

Fire*Wolf grew fearful. He was beginning slowly to realize why the slavers had not followed him into this valley. An eldritch gloom clung to the swamplands near the river. There was too little sound. In any land like this, there should have been a thousand noises: insects, small animals and birds. Here there was none. Silence brooded in the green and dismal gloom.

Swift movement was impossible. Here, in the swamp, the soft ground sucked at his feet, the tangled vegetation gripped his legs and arms, making every stride an effort. He was, so far as he could judge, moving parallel to the river in the approximate direction of the great stone building he had spotted briefly from the valley wall.

He could not say how he first knew something was following him. His nostrils caught no scent, his ears no sound. But his whole instinct, finely honed by years in the Wilderness, told him there was something: and that something getting closer. His mind created pictures of a creature unlike any he had ever known, a beast of cunning and ferocity. He shook his head to try to clear away the vision, but it remained stubbornly.

Fire*Wolf changed direction.

For just the barest instant he thought he might have eluded his pursuer, but then his instincts told him it was following again. It was now closer if anything. He could still hear nothing, see nothing, scent nothing, yet his mind was setting up a clamour close to panic. He had no doubt at all he had become prey to some predator and the creature was closing for the kill.

Fire*Wolf stopped. He was without a weapon of any sort. While the Wilderness Way had taught him many tricks of unarmed combat and survival, he knew that in his present situation he would not last more than minutes against any of the larger beasts of Harn. He looked around and at last found a hefty, broken bough, slick with swamp slime but at least unrotted. He wiped away the slime as best he could and hefted the bough in his strong right hand. A club had never been his favourite weapon, but it was all he had.

Fire*Wolf waited. In time the creature came for him.

It was immense. A swamp reptile of some unknown species, some fifteen feet long from tip of snout to tip of tail and standing almost eight feet tall at the shoulder. The muscular body was armoured with glistening green scales so that it blended with its background almost to perfection. Half-open jaws revealed fangs four inches long. The shortened forelegs ended in vicious, slime-tipped claws. The great head swung slowly side to side, searching. A white, nictating membrane flicked spasmodically across the eyes.

Fire*Wolf and the Swamp Reptile

*A choice for Fire*Wolf. Even with a sword, spear, bow, arrows and heavy armour, the brave Barbarian might have some difficulty in surviving this encounter. Can he possibly survive at all armed only with a makeshift club? There is no dishonour in flight from impossible odds. And yet it has always been Fire*Wolf's nature to attack. In this instance, he may take either option. If Fire*Wolf braves the monster, go to* **19**. *Should he decide to flee, follow his adventures in* **17**.

15

Panting and exhausted, Fire*Wolf halted.

He had left the swamp behind and was now on the banks of the great slow river which, over the course of aeons, had cut this entire valley from the living bedrock.

It was chill here, far colder even than the sodden swamp, and almost as silent. Only the deep sounds of the murky waters reached his ears.

Fire*Wolf rested, shivering, his back against a rock while body and mind slowly recovered from the terrifying encounter. He had, he knew, been lucky. The valley obviously hid greater dangers than he had chosen to imagine – the reason, no doubt, why the slavers had not cared to follow when he made his dramatic escape. To them he had been a dead man from the moment he set foot on the valley floor. It was only a matter of time before the inevitable fate caught up with him.

Perhaps they were right. He had encountered only one living creature so far to be sure, but an eldritch pall clung to this valley like a shroud. Dark forces were at work here and he was ill-equipped to deal with them. He had no right to be here, no business in this place. Every fibre of his body screamed at him to leave – and leave quickly.

What was the fastest route?

Eventually Fire*Wolf stirred himself to action. Using branches, boughs and vines, he lashed himself the crudest of rude rafts and launched it on the river. Still near-naked and unarmed, he stretched his huge, tired body on the makeshift craft, consigned his spirit to the Wilderness gods, and permitted the current to carry him downstream, perhaps to greater dangers, but hopefully beyond this accursed valley.

Silent eyes watched threateningly from undergrowth and thicket as the frail craft rode the murky waters like a piece of errant flotsam. But still nothing moved. The cargo of the raft was meat, but forbidden meat to valley predators, for destiny had marked out this intruder for a darker fate. The craft sailed onwards and we must now move with it to **18**.

16

*(Add one point to Fire*Wolf's* SKILL *figure.)*

Fire*Wolf fled from the scene of the fight.

He was shaken, confused, his mind still reeling from the psychic blasts of the miniature horror. Nightmare visions clung to the edges of his mind. Creatures of the darkness hovered at the edges of his perception, threatening to break through to overwhelm him. Although he knew beyond all doubt the lizard was now dead, the vicious damage it had done to his mind lingered hauntingly.

Fire∗Wolf ran.

Despite his exhaustion, he could not stop. His powerful body crashed through the dense swamp vegetation, heedless of the lacerations it received from razor-edged ferns, the scratches from succulent thorns.

His mind locked in a tight knot of terror, no longer aware of where he ran, Fire∗Wolf stumbled onwards, legs trembling.

And stumbled, luckily, beyond the swamp. Follow him to **15**.

17

Fire∗Wolf froze. There was still the possibility the creature might not see him. But then the great head turned in his direction, the cold eyes locked on his own. At once, Fire∗Wolf moved, breaking through the tangled undergrowth as quickly as the swampy ground would permit him, desperately searching for firmer ground where the strength of his legs could carry him swiftly from the beast.

There was no sound behind him, but a glance over his shoulder confirmed the reptile had lunged in his direction, maw gaping, and was now pressing him close.

Fire∗Wolf's chances of escape are slim. Roll two dice. Score 2 to 4 and go to **15**. *Score 5 to 12 and go to* **21**.

18

Fire*Wolf awoke with a start, only now realizing he had allowed himself to fall into a fitful doze.

The steady, slow, hypnotic movement of his makeshift raft had stopped. He looked around. Time and his little vessel hung suspended in the centre of a gloomy lake. Dank, twisted, fungus-ridden trees overhung the distant banks, their leaves showing leprous whites and greys in the moonlight.

Moonlight! He had not merely dozed, but slept and slept soundly. The gods alone knew for how long, or how far his craft had travelled. But he had halted now. No current tugged at his raft. It sat motionless as a mariner on a sea of glass.

All around him, the stillness was profound.

Only to the south where a fogbank roilled, creating ghoul and demon visions, was anything revealed to the imaginative eye. Even as he watched, the mist parted briefly to reveal the stark grey-black outlines of a great stone keep towering by the water's edge.

At once the raft began to move again, in the direction of the fogbank. Fire*Wolf jumped to his feet, balancing precariously.

*In his present frame of mind, Fire*Wolf might opt to jump overboard and swim, to take his chances in the tangled forest. Or curiosity might impel him to approach the great stone castle, enshrouded by the rolling mists. The choice now is no longer his, but rather yours. To swim the lake, go to* **22**. *To approach the castle, go to* **28**.

19

The Warrior Cry of the Wilderness rang out across the sodden swamplands as Fire*Wolf flung himself upon the monster, swinging his makeshift club at the creature's gaping maw.

It was a fine blow, well-timed and well-aimed. He knew this with a fighter's instinct the moment the full power of his massive body was released. The club swung true.

And missed!

Momentum carried Fire*Wolf in a half circle, causing him to stumble. But he recovered quickly. Had the monster moved? It did not seem to have moved.

He swung again.

This time there could be no mistake. He watched the heavy bough pass through the body of the creature as if it were so much thin air.

Howling in amazement and frustration, Fire*Wolf struck again . . . and the monster vanished! For an instant he froze, dumbfounded. Then a tiny movement near his foot caused him to look down. A miniature replica of the creature skeetered towards him, scarcely more than seven inches long.

He might have let the little lizard live, but some blind instinct brought his arm down with the club. The creature jumped nimbly to one side and a soundless blast of mental energy exploded within Fire*Wolf's brain.

*Whether it be seven inches long or fifteen feet, the being Fire*Wolf faces is a monster indeed. Perhaps* *the most deadly denizen of the Swamps of Voltan, the venomous Illusion Lizard has been equipped by nature with certain strange and dangerous abilities. These, and its combat statistics, are listed on page 248 to help you calculate the outcome of this encounter. If Fire*Wolf dies, turn to* **13**. *If Fire*Wolf survives, move on to* **16**.

20

Baldar placed a skinny, mocking foot on Fire*Wolf's broad chest, grinning down at the big Barbarian as he lay on the rough ground. 'There, my fine angry friend. Even youth and rage are no match for experience. But take heart: I was a practised fighter in my early days and the skills are never lost.' He removed his foot and held out a hand to help Fire*Wolf upright. 'I hear it is the custom of the Wilderness Barbarians to grant a man a favour if he bests you in combat. Is that true?'

'True enough,' Fire*Wolf admitted sourly. He dusted himself off, no longer angry at the hermit, but angry at himself that he had allowed the other to best him.

'In that case,' Baldar said, 'I shall claim a favour from you. Will you run an errand for me to Belgardium?'

'Belgardium?' Fire*Wolf asked. 'The name is unfamiliar to me.'

'As all civilized names must be unfamiliar to you, Fungus Feeder,' Baldar said shortly. 'It is a place where once I had my roots. Come into the cave and I shall tell you why I wish you to go there.'

He turned and walked towards the cave mouth. Bound

by the Wilderness tradition, Fire*Wolf had no option but to follow.

Go to **144**.

21

Fire*Wolf stumbled.

On the instant the lizard was upon him, soundlessly. He could see the massive fangs, the gleaming scales, the rending talons. Yet he heard nothing, scented nothing, and felt nothing other than a pinprick on his thigh.

Fire*Wolf reached up in a desperate attempt to defend himself; and his hands grasped thin air. The vision of the monster wavered, faded, then Fire*Wolf plunged into a pit of darkness.

Go to **13**.

22

Fire*Wolf dived off the raft without an instant's hesitation. The waters of the lake embraced him like a dank cloak. He ignored the chill and struck out strongly for the shore.

Fire*Wolf was a strong swimmer. He had learned the art in the great subterranean lakes of the Deep Wilderness, chill and forbidding waters that no sun had ever seen. Yet for all his strength and skill, he quickly found that in this placid, moonlit lake, something was wrong. He should have reached the shore in minutes, yet, swimming strongly, the shore still seemed distant as ever.

After a time he changed direction. It made no difference. The shore seemed just as remote. He changed direction again, with similar results. A worm of fear began to crawl within his stomach.

*What black sorcery is afoot here? Roll two dice to determine Fire*Wolf's fate. Score 2 to 6 and go to* **25**. *Score 7 to 12 and go to* **29**.

23

A flare of raw, blue-white energy leapt jarring through his arm to engulf him.

He felt his soul spin within his body, faster and faster until his mind reeled and his senses expanded to embrace the entire cosmos.

Behind him, great stones seemed to move in some gargantuan, stately dance. Voices gibbered in his ears, then resolved themselves into one voice. It spoke to him in cultured, measured tones, silkily confident with the power of ages past behind its words:

'Too soon, Barbarian. Thou wert not ready!'

And then he tumbled into darkness.

Go to **13**.

24

His half-formed plan had been to snatch the sword, permitting his momentum to carry him beyond the open chamber. But as his hand closed on the hilt, a surge of sudden power locked his entire body into immobility.

It seemed he stood there for an age within the open chamber formed by the great stones before a silky voice spoke clearly in his mind:

24

'Welcome, Fire*Wolf. Welcome, crude Barbarian. Welcome to your destiny.'
'Who are you?' Fire*Wolf gasped.

'I am Doombringer,' said the voice. 'I am Lifepreserver. I am a demon from the deepest Pits of Hell. I am an angel from the highest Battlements of Heaven. I am Joy. I am Sorrow. I am your sword, Fire*Wolf. Name me what you will.'

The blade shivered, vibrated and sang in his hand. He felt a surge of unholy power flow through his blood.

'You are my sword?' he whispered.

'Yours by right of courage, by right of luck, by right of destiny,' the voice said. 'I was forged for you – and others like you – before the dawn of time. Fear not, Barbarian, for I will serve you well and charge you little.'

'Charge?' echoed Fire*Wolf.

'The services of such as I are never free. There is a token payment which must be exacted.'

'Then tell me what it is!' growled Fire*Wolf, at last recovering his natural equilibrium.

He was surrounded momentarily by green light and in the instant knew the history of his sword.

*To learn what Fire*Wolf discovered of Doombringer, including the fighting stats of this sentient blade, turn to page 249. Then go on to* **26**.

25

With growing desperation, Fire*Wolf changed direction again.

And again.

Nothing worked. The waters of the dark lake clung to him like an animal, drawing the warmth from his body in a way that natural water never did.

He swam and swam until he thought his heart must burst.

The shore was no nearer. . .

Go to **13**.

26

Desperately, Fire*Wolf dashed the sword to the ground. At once, it was in his hand again.

'Ah, no, Barbarian,' the smooth voice echoed softly in his mind, 'there is no getting rid of me. We are one now. I am your Destiny, Fire*Wolf. You are nothing without me and we may not be parted, now or ever, until your Destiny is fulfilled . . . or until your death.'

Scowling, Fire*Wolf stuck the sword into his belt. He felt stronger now than at any time since he had entered this accursed valley. Nonetheless, he loathed the realization that this was a parasitic strength, lifeblood leeched by the Demonsword from ancient enemies. 'Stay quiet now,' he growled. 'Stay out of my mind. I may have to use you, but I see no reason why I should have to listen to you as well!'

'As you wish,' the silken tones responded amiably.

26

Then he felt the presence slip from his mind and was the cleaner for it.

Fire*Wolf started to move from the trilithon chamber. A small stone beneath his foot caused him to stumble. He put out an instinctive hand, reaching out to save himself, and touched one of the sidestones.

The forest clearing dissolved in a soundless burst of golden light.

Turn at once to **27**.

THE PRISONER

27

He was in a stone-lined room, a cell of some description. Grey light filtered in from a small barred window high overhead. There was a stout oakwood door, tight shut, up three stone steps to the northern wall (or as near as he could judge to be the northern wall).

The chamber itself was cold, but dry and clean. It was unfurnished and virtually bare excepting for three iron levers set into the wall beside the door and a worn, almost featureless bronze casting of some ancient, monstrous god set upon a granite pedestal in the centre of the floor. A bronze plaque on the pedestal bore the fading remnants of an inscription. Fire*Wolf glanced at it, squinting slightly to make out the lines and discovered it was written in the ancient runic script of prehistoric Harn. Faint memories of shaman lessons in the script nudged at the edges of his mind, but he knew he would have to work hard to decipher the inscription, working virtually from first principles.

Meanwhile, there were more important mysteries to be solved. How he came to be here, for one thing. More importantly, how he could get out. Without much optimism, he crossed the room, mounted the three stone steps and tried the door. It was, as he had expected, locked. He glanced at the three levers, wondering at their purpose. To open the door, perhaps? That seemed the obvious answer, but perchance it was *too* obvious. Such devices were sometimes known to trigger traps.

Where was he?

Short of leaving the chamber – and he still did not know how that might be accomplished – there was only one way of finding out. He moved to the wall with the window and examined it closely. The masonry was old, the mortar surface crumbling. He removed Doombringer from his belt and laid the sword carefully on the floor, then, using toes and fingers in the Wilderness Way, climbed the wall like a fly.

He reached the tiny window and looked out through the bars. The scene was gloomily familiar: the brooding lake on which his makeshift raft had so recently sailed. So he now knew where he was. But how had he come so abruptly to this chamber? What forces had imprisoned him? He tried the window bars and found them firm. Carefully he climbed back down again.

Fire*Wolf squatted for a moment, great head hung forward, hair falling like a tawny mane over his handsome features. He needed to think.

Thinking is not, of course, an option our man of action particularly enjoys. You may, perhaps, help him by examining the possibilities. He might, for example, take time to translate the runic inscription on the bronze plaque of the ancient god. If so, follow him to **30**. *Alternatively, he might be tempted to try*

Fire*Wolf approaches the keep

his luck with the iron levers which may provide a method of unlocking the door. If so, go to **33**.

28

The fogbank closed around him and for a moment he might have been alone in the universe, totally cut off from any semblance of reality. But then the current quickened, carrying him beyond the mists to beach his raft gently on the shore.

Fire*Wolf stepped off warily. He was at the end of a rough stone causeway. The great keep he had seen earlier now towered gloomily before him, less than two hundred yards away. From so close, it seemed a building of gargantuan proportions. Even from the lakeside he could see that huge blocks had been cut and polished to form the castle walls. The architectural form spoke of another age. Irresistibly, Fire*Wolf's mind jumped back to a portion of the great myth cycle sung by the shamans of his tribe, the part which told of the days when giants lived on earth.

With no better alternative, he walked the causeway. As he drew close, the castle took on a different aspect. From the lakeside it had only seemed huge. Now he could see it was enormous but derelict. There had been a moat once; but now it was no more than a deep, stone-lined ditch empty of water and part overgrown by grass. A drawbridge spanned the ditch, its timbers cracked and rotted so that he was forced to cross it with great care to prevent himself falling through.

On the other side, an iron grid portcullis hung neither up nor down, its ancient mechanisms hopelessly jammed by rust. Fire*Wolf passed beneath it easily, along a short stone-flagged tunnel with murder holes cut into its roof, and through a broken gateway into a wide, overgrown reception yard.

Fire*Wolf stopped, fighting back the disappointment that had been growing in him. If he had hoped for help in leaving the valley, he would not find it here. This castle had lain deserted for many generations. But there was still the possibility he might find weapons, perhaps even armour which had escaped the ravages of time. When a man was naked and unarmed in a hostile world, such possibilities assumed a great importance.

He looked around him. Several archways and various doorways led off the courtyard. A number of the latter were broken, hanging on rotted hinges. Beyond some of them he could see the remnants of ancient stables, broken roofs admitting the ghostly illumination of the moonlight. The remnants of the stalls told him that if giants had built this place, they had not lived here: the stables were for horses of normal proportions.

Fire*Wolf moved forward and at once saw the sword.

It lay, no more than a pace or two away from him, half-hidden in the grass and cleavers tangle which had overtaken the yard flags beneath his feet. It was a slim blade, lighter than his usual preference, but despite the ages it must have lain here, it remained bright and free from rust. The polished, blue-black metal glinting in the moonlight was unfamiliar to him. Tiny lights, like distant stars, glinted in its depths. The handle seemed to be carved from obsidian.

Fire*Wolf discovers Doombringer

Slim blade or no, it was a weapon, and one which Fire*Wolf desperately needed. Without a moment's hesitation, he reached down to pick up the sword.

*And in doing so, brave, rash Fire*Wolf set in motion an inevitable wheel of Destiny. Roll two dice for him now and compare the result with his* LUCK *figure. If the total is greater than the* LUCK *figure, go to* **23**. *If the total is less than the* LUCK *figure, go to* **31**.

29

He swam for an eternity, it seemed, but finally, near exhausted, felt his feet touch bottom and clambered up on to the shore. A mossy bank extended no more than a few feet before the tangled, leprous forest formed a near impenetrable barrier.

Fire*Wolf rested for a time, then rose to push into the forest. The stillness, so characteristic of this valley, was profound here. It was as if the world was waiting . . . or had died. He would have given much for a broadsword, or even a dagger, and even more for some protection for his body which was now slick with blood from a hundred tiny wounds and scratches.

Blindly, not knowing where he was going and caring less, Fire*Wolf pressed deeper into the forest, but was eventually forced to stop. The moonlight would not penetrate here and even his keen night vision could not give him sight of the ground at his feet. He chose a large tree, partly by feel, partly by its upper silhouette against the sky, climbed into its sturdy lower branches then, wedging himself in a fork, settled down to fitful sleep while he awaited sunrise.

29

He found, when he awoke, that he was perched overlooking a clearing. If he had stumbled just a few feet more, he would have been able to reach it the night before. What he saw within the clearing filled him with superstitious awe. To the west, three huge stones had been set – two uprights and a capstone – while circling the clearing were more great stones, perhaps twenty in all, towering like giant sentries against the dense backdrop of the forest. He knew at once that he had stumbled on a place of ancient power. Shaman priests in the deeper warrens of his rock village spoke of such places in awed whispers. They had been established aeons ago by the Great Old Ones to work the most potent of their many magics. The shamans called them the Ringstone Rounds and some were supposed to have been set even in the Wilderness itself, although Fire*Wolf knew of no one who had ever claimed to have seen one.

Fire*Wolf stretched stiff muscles, then climbed down slowly from the tree. Was this, he wondered, the secret of the silent valley? According to the shamans, some of the Rounds still generated their ancient power. Who knew now what results such power might have wrought on a place over the centuries? Fire*Wolf listened, but heard nothing, opened up his senses, but felt nothing. Nonetheless he felt nervous. The big Barbarian had no fondness of magic. He was, before all, a fighting man and the mysteries frightened and confused him.

He was also, unfortunately, a fighting man cursed with a strong tendency to curiosity, so, after considerable hesitation, he found himself moving cautiously into the clearing.

The stones looked old as time, huge, rough-hewn granite pillars, none less than twice his own six feet, set upright, some straight, some angled, at intervals of a few yards around the circle. Eventually he summoned sufficient courage to pass between them, and was profoundly relieved when nothing happened. The ground within the circle sloped gently upwards towards the centre, like a shallow, inverted dish. His Wilderness-trained eyes caught traces of ancient fires here, but no indication of any human visitor for many generations.

He moved cautiously across the circle, taking care to touch nothing, nor to pass too close to any stone. Still nervous as a kitten, he walked beyond the circle proper and approached the trilithon to the west. These were the greatest stones of all, slabs set to form an open chamber in which, he noticed, both grass and lichens had taken on a distinctly bluish tinge. He had half turned to move away again when an errant ray of morning sunlight picked up the glint of metal.

Fire*Wolf stopped. The sword was almost completely hidden in the blue-green grass within the chamber formed by the trilithon. And though he was certain no one had passed this way for years – perhaps for centuries – what he could see of the metal was bright, clean, rust-free.

For what seemed eternity, he stood staring, locked in indecision. Here was the weapon he so desperately needed. But dare he claim it? To do so would mean entering the trilithon chamber and that thought filled him with a nameless dread.

Eventually, cautiously, he took a single step forward and was encouraged when no instant doom befell him.

Should he run in and snatch the sword swiftly, or creep with great caution to steal it away before the Great Powers noticed him?

He took another step, so that now he stood at the very mouth of the chamber. He could see more of the weapon now. It was a slimmer blade than he would have preferred, forged from some unfamiliar blue-black metal, with a delicately carved hilt of what appeared to be obsidian. Tiny lights, like distant stars, glinted in its depths.

Fire*Wolf remained immobile for a moment, then, impelled by some half-conscious urge, plunged within the chamber and snatched up the sword.

*And so, on the instant, the die was cast. And now you too must cast a die on brave Fire*Wolf's behalf. This time, however, you should roll two dice and compare your score with his* LUCK *figure. If you rolled a score less than the figure for his* LUCK *go to* **24**. *If the score is higher than his* LUCK *figure, go to* **23**.

30

Fire*Wolf bent over the bronze plaque, straining to discern the faded outlines of the ancient runes. It might be no more than a salutation to the Elder God, but some errant instinct, fine-honed by his years in the Wilderness, whispered that it might be more.

Carefully he traced the outlines with his finger, memorizing the faint tracks as the shamans had taught him, until at last the whole inscription was written clearly in his mind. Or almost the whole inscription, for two characters were faded beyond all recognition.

The inscription looked like this:

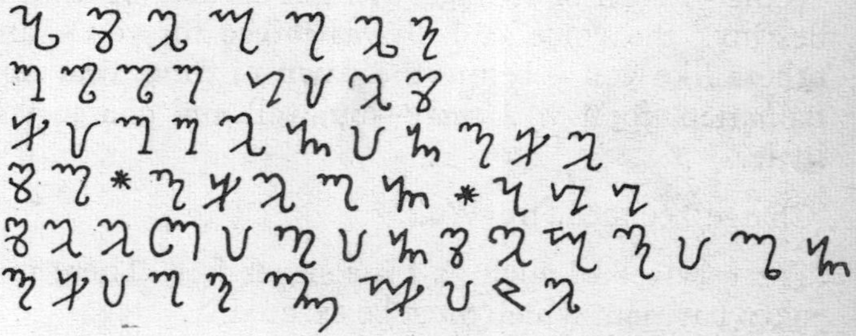

A clue to Fire∗Wolf's fate, perhaps? Or nothing at all? Perhaps you already hold the key. Perhaps no key exists. If your attempts to solve the riddle of the runes come to nothing, then you have no option other than returning to **27** *and attempting to escape some other way.*

31

As his eager hand closed on the obsidian hilt, a jolt of power coursed through his arm and into his muscular body. At once a silken smooth voice echoed in his mind:

'Welcome, Fire∗Wolf. Welcome, crude Barbarian. Welcome to your Destiny.'

'Who are you?' Fire∗Wolf gasped.

'I am Doombringer,' said the voice. 'I am Lifepreserver. I am a demon from the deepest Pits of Hell. I am an angel from the highest Battlements of Heaven. I am Joy. I am Sorrow. I am your sword, Fire∗Wolf. Name me what you will.'

The blade shivered, vibrated and sang in his hand. He felt a surge of unholy power flow through his blood.

'You are my sword?' he whispered.

'Yours by right of courage, by right of luck, by right of destiny,' the voice said. 'I was forged for you – and others like you – before the dawn of time. Fear not, Barbarian, for I will serve you well and charge you little.'

'Charge?' echoed Fire*Wolf.

'The services of such as I are never free. There is a token payment which must be exacted.'

'Then tell me what it is!' growled Fire*Wolf, at last recovering his natural equilibrium.

In a moment, he was surrounded by green light and in the instant knew the history of his sword.

> *To learn what Fire*Wolf discovered of Doombringer, including the fighting stats of this sentient blade, turn to page 249 Then go on to* **32**.

32

Fire*Wolf stood stunned. His soul revolted against the very concept of such a sword. As a fighting man he had done his share of killing, but they had been clean kills, always in self-defence, self-preservation or in defence of something he held dear. To kill for the sake of another's life essence was a hellish concept.

On impulse he flung the weapon from him. And at once it was in his hand.

'Ah no, Fire*Wolf,' the silken voice murmured in his mind, 'we are one now, you and I. Our fates are intertwined and there is no ridding yourself of me except by death.'

'Think you that?' roared Fire*Wolf in a sudden rage. 'Think you that?' He smashed the blade furiously against the nearest wall, seeking to shatter the metal on the stone.

But as the sword blade struck, a whirlpool of green light sprang up from the stone and enveloped him completely.

*What sorcery has Fire*Wolf's impulsive action unleashed? Go to* **27** *to discover the answer.*

33

Fire*Wolf examined the levers. Each was less than a foot long, cast from iron and surprisingly rust-free. They were set in a narrow iron frame recessed into the wall itself. After careful study, he was convinced that they linked with some mechanism inside.

Would they open the door? Or trigger a trap? He had no way of knowing. But nor had he any other way of leaving this prison. Better, perhaps, to die in a trap than waste away slowly from starvation. He determined to try the mechanism.

Cautiously, Fire*Wolf tested each lever. It seemed each moved independently and each could be pushed upwards or pulled downwards. There was no side to side movement.

A moment's calculation indicated that there were seven possible positions for the levers. But which to try?

*Fire*Wolf is faced with an impossible decision. The right move may free him, the wrong move may kill him. There is nothing to guide him, yet a choice* *must be made. The different positions for the levers are shown below. Consider carefully and make your choice.*

Key
ù = lever up.
/ = lever down.

ùùù	= go to **38**.
ùù/	= go to **41**.
ù//	= go to **45**.
ù/ù	= go to **49**.
//ù	= go to **53**.
///	= go to **57**.
/ù/	= go to **61**.

34

Why hesitate? There was nothing to draw him back to the chamber beneath. If he was to find a way out of his prison, Fire*Wolf must face whatever risks arose. He began to crawl along the narrow little tunnel.

The crawlspace twisted and turned so frequently that he was hard put to hold on to his sense of direction: or to judge its length. But it did not seem long before he reached a dead end. His questing fingers explored what appeared to be a wall of solid stone.

But a wall here made no sense whatsoever. There had to be a secret opening of some description. Fire*Wolf began to search.

*Roll two dice against Fire*Wolf's combined* LUCK *and* SKILL *figures. If you score below this total, go to*

36. *Score above and Fire∗Wolf's only option is to return to the prison room at* **27** *or* **33**.

35

Fire∗Wolf searched the walls.

At first he thought the inscription must have been mistaken, for the stonework, ancient as it was, remained fine, with no sign at all of any secret opening.

Then, quite unexpectedly, he found it. No more than a hairline crack, but once discovered enough to investigate so that, inevitably, he found the catch. The mechanism was simple but astonishingly effective. A light pressure in the correct direction and an entire slab slid away. Behind it was darkness, but for Fire∗Wolf at that moment it was as inviting as bright sunlight. It was a way out of his prison.

Mindless of what might lie in store, he plunged in. The secret door closed silently behind him.

Perhaps rash, but perfectly understandable in the circumstances. Follow Fire∗Wolf now to **39**.

36

His questing fingers found a crack. By following it carefully in the darkness he discovered a small indentation. A light pressure and suddenly the wall gave way inwards, swinging back on well-oiled hinges.

Fire∗Wolf half fell forward. He was in a smallish chamber, a ten foot cube windowless but lighted by a single oil lamp. What he saw by that light sent his hand reaching mindlessly for the foul Doomsword at his side.

37

Facing him was a large, wild-eyed, red-haired and half-naked Barbarian, smelling of the Wilderness but without the typical look. This creature too was armed with a slim-bladed blue-black sword.

It took Fire*Wolf an instant of bewilderment to realize the truth. He was facing *himself*! The barbarian was his double in every way – right down to the small graze on his knee where he had scraped it on the floor of the crawlspace.

'Who are you?' Fire*Wolf gasped.

For answer, the other gave a high-pitched, melodious trill and launched himself forward.

*An ancient legend states that when a man meets with his doppelgänger, his exact double, then that man is fated for immediate death. Can Fire*Wolf face this weird shape-shifter so like him in every way but speech? In resolving the conflict, remember that the doppelgänger's fighting stats are identical to those of Fire*Wolf. The only difference is his sword which, while it looks like Doombringer, has no sorcerous properties and functions only as a normal sword. There is no avoiding this fight. If the doppelgänger wins, go to* **13**. *If Fire*Wolf wins, go to* **37**.

37

(Add one SKILL *point to Fire*Wolf's total.)*

As Fire*Wolf stared down at his own corpse, he saw the body changing. It grew slimmer, elongating in a manner that wrenched the mind, changing colour to a leprous grey until it became something other than human.

Fire*Wolf shuddered and turned away. If this was a sample of what lay in store for him within this castle, then the sooner he found his way out the better. Now the fight was over, he had time to examine the chamber properly. There was no door other than the one by which he had entered and a careful search of walls, floor and ceiling revealed no secret openings. Had the creature lived here? And if so, how? Or had it merely hidden here, waiting for him? But how, then, could it tell he would ever find the chamber?

The whole mystery smelt of foul magics and Fire*Wolf was content to leave it alone. He backed from the chamber, sealing the secret door behind him and made his way back along the crawlspace to his original prison room.

Go to **33** *and continue experimenting with the levers or return to* **27** *and reconsider Fire*Wolf's position from that perspective.*

38

Fire*Wolf pushed the first lever upwards, then the second, then the third.

They moved easily and silently, locking lightly in place with a discernible click.

He waited . . .

Nothing. Nothing happened. Return to **33** *and try again.*

LORD OF THE VALLEY

39

He was in a narrow, stone-lined room, scarcely more than six feet wide, so that by stretching out his hands, he might have touched the walls on either side. It should have been pitch dark here, but a species of luminous mould clung to the stone so that when his eyes adjusted, he could see dimly, but well enough.

The corridor ran straight for close on fifty feet, then ended in a flight of worn stone steps descending into stygian darkness.

Fire*Wolf hesitated. Not even the luminous mould grew in this pit to give him light. Should he risk the stairs in total darkness?

His deliberations were short. To turn back now meant at best a return to the prison chamber . . . and at worst there would be no means of opening the secret panel from this side. It was go forward or nothing.

All the same, he drew his sword.

As he placed an uncertain foot on the topmost step, the suave tones of Doombringer echoed in his mind: 'Must you fumble in the darkness like a blind beggar, Fire*Wolf? It is in my power to give you light.'

'Then do it!' Fire*Wolf growled, nervousness overcoming his instinctive aversion to the accursed sword.

'There is a small payment, fearful Barbarian. A token only. . .'

Fire*Wolf froze. Who knew what foul price this blade might extract. 'Payment?' he asked.

'No more than three units of your life essence,' Doombringer whispered. 'Much less than you might lose should you meet some adversary in the darkness.'

'My life essence?' Fire*Wolf hissed.

'Unfortunately,' Doombringer murmured in the depths of his mind, 'once given, those three units may never be regained. Not by time or magic or healing. But the bargain remains fair. Three units only and I shall give you light now and in the future whenever it is necessary.'

Fire*Wolf hesitated, locked in indecision.

As well he might. Three LIFE POINTS *seems a small price – and yet those* LIFE POINTS *will be gone forever. Who knows in this land of constant dangers when three* LIFE POINTS *might make the final difference between life and death? And who knows what further tributes this accursed sword might subsequently demand for services? Nonetheless, a source of light might in itself mean the difference between life and death. A dilemma – and one immediately beyond the judgement of our brave Barbarian. Thus you must make the choice for him. Should you decide to invest the* LIFE POINTS, *go to* **46**. *But if you feel it better that Fire*Wolf proceed in darkness, go to* **54**.

40

At last he reached the bottom of the steps. The flame-sword in his hand illuminated a large, circular, high-ceilinged chamber, rather like a shaft, or, more likely, the cellar of a round tower, for there was in fact a spiral flight of metal steps at the far side of the room.

But Fire*Wolf's attention was taken instantly by something else – or rather by two other things. The first was a series of open pits, each some five feet square, which were set at intervals along the floor like some monstrous distortion of a chequerboard design. The other, demanding more immediate attention, was the night-black creature crouching no more than ten feet distant from him, lithe muscles tensed as if to spring. While bipedal and vaguely manlike in appearance, it was covered head to foot in sleek black fur and the head and features were of feline cast. Amber orbs regarded him suspiciously and the creature's lips curled back in a sudden, throaty snarl.

Oh dear, oh dear! What an uncommonly difficult situation for the Barbarian. He is facing a pantherine – one of the swiftest and most deadly predators in Harn. No supernatural creature this: merely a jet-black feline of high intelligence, rudimentary speech and vile disposition, in appearance like a cross between a panther and an ape. As always, you will find the creature's stats listed on *page 248.* *But before you begin to calculate the outcome of this encounter, two points must be made. The first is that there is a small chance Fire*Wolf can avoid a fight. Compare the pantherine's* CHARM *figure with that of Fire*Wolf. If Fire*Wolf's figure is higher, then our Barbarian may be permitted one double dice roll, multiplied by eight,* *against his own* CHARM *figure. If he scores below that figure, then the pantherine will immediately abandon its attack. But should Fire*Wolf fail, the fight is on. In this event, each blow that Fire*Wolf strikes must be accompanied by a second roll of a single dice. Unless he scores above 1 with this roll, you may take it he has fallen down a pit. Should he fall, go direct to* **42**. *Should the pantherine retreat, go to* **68**. *Should the pantherine kill him, go to* **13**. *Should he kill the pantherine, go to* **62**.

41

Fire*Wolf pushed the first and second levers upwards, took a deep breath and pulled the third lever down.

He waited.

Nothing. Nothing happened. Return to **33** *and try again.*

42

Fire*Wolf gagged.

His fall of almost fifteen feet had ended without injury on something soft, but the sweet scent of putrefaction embraced him like a sullen fog. Hastily he scrambled upright, gasping for breath as the foul odour seeped into his lungs. He had, he found, dropped his sword when he fell, presumably in the chamber above. But there was at least some light here in the pit, a cancerous green luminescence generated by microbes and crawling insects, sufficient to show him a scene from nightmare.

The pit was full of rotting corpses.

Decomposing flesh hung in ghastly strips from bleaching bones. Mouldering rags encased the horrid remnants of

Fire*Wolf and the Pantherine

what had once been men, and military men to judge by the rusting swords and helmets.

A soldiers' cemetery?

The decaying evidence of a massacre?

The corpses *moved*! They undulated gently, like a sullen sea. Small, slow, unthreatening movements of skull heads and bony fingers, the gradual turning of half-rotted eyeballs in cavernous sockets. Arms reaching out towards him with the dread uncertainty of a terminal gasp.

For the first time in his life, Fire*Wolf knew real fear. In revulsion that was close to panic, he drew back and looked around to find, with profound relief, that footholds had been cut at intervals in several places into the pit walls.

Fire*Wolf leaped and climbed as if the demons of Deep Hell were after him. Better a thousand pantherines than the grisly horrors of this tomb.

The undead creatures made no move to follow him, merely stretched, stared and oozed in his direction, soundless as a midnight graveyard.

He neared the lip of the pit and found, set in a niche close by his hand-hold, a lamp and tinderbox. Despite the horror below him and the danger above, the seduction of good honest light proved too strong and, balanced on the wall, he gripped the lamp and struck the tinder.

The yellow glow of fine oil reached out to dispel the gloom. At once, the gentle movement of the corpses changed. They began to drag themselves upright, settling helmets on flayed skulls, gripping rusted swords with skeletal fingers. One after one, the undead warriors searched out the footholds in the walls.

With a sound close to a whimper, Fire*Wolf scrambled up the last remaining few feet of the pit.

Immediately, at the top of the pit, he faced the snarling fangs not of the single pantherine he had so recently attacked, but of a ringed pantherine pack, a dozen or more, black demons poised to spring.

*Unwelcome though the interruption may be at this point, it must be here admitted that Fire*Wolf, in his extremity, contemplated suicide. Should you decide he turned this thought to action, go to* **13**. *If, on the other hand, you consider some near-dead spark of courage nonetheless sustained him, turn to* **58**.

43

With no indication of how he got there, Fire*Wolf found himself standing near the doorway of a large, rectangular chamber, musty smelling but well lit by sunlight streaming from high windows.

Even at first glance, he recognized the Wilderness shaman's description of an alchemist's laboratory. Wooden benches ran down the centre of the room. Shelves along the walls housed retorts, crucibles, vials and leather-bound tomes. To his right loomed the blackened structure of a furnace.

But it was a laboratory long disused. Equipment on the benches lay toppled or broken. The furnace was cold and a thin layer of dust lay everywhere. Behind him, the doorway lay half open, a rotted timber door hanging drunkenly from one hinge. Three further doors, in rather better repair, led out of the laboratory. There was no sign at all of the spiral staircase.

*A multiplicity of choices for Fire*Wolf. He may, for example, decide to explore this disused laboratory thoroughly: in which case turn to* **47**. *He might simply turn and leave through the broken door, in which case turn to* **52**. *Or he might care to try any one of the three further exit doors. To the right, go to* **56**. *To the left, go to* **60**. *Straight ahead, go to* **63**.

44

Fire*Wolf awoke to sunlight in a strange soft bed. He was in a bright, airy room, newly cleaned by the smell, and pleasantly furnished in stark contrast with anything else he had so far seen in this accursed castle.

He was naked. Even his loincloth had been removed. But he lay between crisp cream linen sheets on a mattress that could only have been filled with duck-down. A bowl of fresh fruit – apples, plums, pears – sat on a small bedside table near his hand. Propped against the table was the Doomsword.

Fire*Wolf glanced around him. This room at least had every indication of being lived in. Perhaps he was no longer in the castle. He had no means of telling how long he had been unconscious, although the sunlight suggested it must be several hours at least.

He sat up and found himself weak – too weak to stand. He was, he discovered, ravenously hungry. His hand reached for the fruit, then instinct stopped him. Instead he gripped the Doomsword, allowing its foul energy to flow into his body.

'You were wise,' the suave voice echoed in his mind. 'The plums are poisoned.'

'Poisoned? How do you know?'

'I have more talents than you realize, Fire*Wolf. You may eat the apples or the pears, although the apples are a little under ripe.'

'Where am I?'

'Who can say?' the Doomsword answered smoothly. 'I sense we are still in the castle, although it seems changed.'

'How long have I slept?' asked Fire*Wolf.

'Now there,' said the Doomsword, 'lies a mystery, for I find the question meaningless and I know not why.'

Scowling, Fire*Wolf set down the blade and rose naked from the bed. He was half way across the room to the window when the door of the chamber opened. He turned to find himself looking into the startled blue eyes of the most beautiful woman he had ever seen. The blue eyes travelled downwards from his face. Fire*Wolf leaped back to the bed and drew a sheet around him, flushing.

'You seem somewhat recovered,' the woman remarked drily. Her voice was melodious, her accent that of the nobility.

'Thank you, yes,' Fire*Wolf stuttered. 'But who are you? And where am I?'

'I am your hostess, lately your nurse. My name is Arcana. And as to where you are, you are in my home.'

'But how did I get here?'

'All in good time,' Arcana told him. 'First you must rest and recover fully. When that is done, there will be time enough for questions.' She glanced towards the Doomsword. 'We permit no weapons here, but I was unable to separate that one from you.'

'It is a sorcerous blade,' Fire*Wolf murmured. 'It will not leave my side.' The mention of the Doomsword brought something to his mind. The lady was beautiful, but the plums were poisoned. All was not as it seemed.

Arcana moved gracefully to sit on the edge of the bed.

'First,' she said, 'you must grow strong.' She reached out to the fruit bowl and selected a pear for him.

Fire*Wolf took it cautiously. 'Will you not join me, My Lady? A plum perhaps?'

For just the barest instant she appeared to hesitate, then smiled. 'If it pleases you . . .' And the slim white hand reached out to take a plum.

'No!' Fire*Wolf exclaimed as she made to bite it. He gripped her wrist.

'No? What strange custom is this, Barbarian?'

Fire*Wolf flushed again. 'The plums . . . the plums . . .'

She extricated herself from his grip and popped the plum in her mouth. 'Not at their peak,' she said.

Angrily, Fire*Wolf bit the pear. It too was sweet, free from poison. Why had the Doomsword lied?

'What is your name?'

'Fire*Wolf,' he muttered, still puzzled and uneasy.

'A handsome warrior name for a handsome warrior,' Arcana smiled. She reached out to touch the bare flesh of his breast. Her hand was cool and the touch sent shivers along his spine. 'If you do not think me forward for saying so,' she added.

'No. No. Not at all.' Beside him, on the edge of his perception, he thought he heard the Doomsword hum.

The blue eyes locked in on his own. 'I am only one of several women in this place and it is our custom to speak plainly of matters which are sometimes cast in convoluted terms. May I speak plainly to you now, Fire*Wolf, without offering offence?'

Fire*Wolf swallowed. 'Yes. Yes, of course.'

'I should like to remain with you,' Arcana told him. 'Will you accept me?'

> *Is there a decision to be made? Fire*Wolf's blood was always eager and the Lady Arcana is by far the most beautiful he has ever seen. With strength borrowed from the Doomsword – the lying Doomsword – he has more than sufficient energy for the jousts of passion. But Fire*Wolf is you and you are Fire*Wolf and consequently the decision must be yours. Should he answer yes, go to* **70**. *A boorish refusal will take you to* **64**.

45

Fire*Wolf pushed the leftmost lever upwards then, with two quick, decisive movements, pulled the remaining two down.

At once he found himself falling as the slab beneath his feet dropped in with a crash. With lightning reflexes he tried to seize the levers again, but his fingers missed them by a hairsbreadth. He plummeted downwards into darkness for perhaps fifteen or twenty feet then landed with a bone-jarring crash on a stone floor.

(*Is Fire*Wolf injured? Roll two dice against his* LUCK *figure. Score below the* LUCK *figure and he is shaken but unhurt. Score higher than the* LUCK *figure and he has been injured. Roll two more dice and deduct the total from his current* LIFE POINTS.)

Injured or no, Fire*Wolf quickly realized he had had an extremely lucky escape. As his eyes adjusted to the gloom, he discovered he was not alone in the pit. Impaled on a vicious spike – a spike which he himself had only just missed – was a bleached white human skeleton, the sole remains of some poor unfortunate who had also found the lethal combination of the levers. Clutched in the skeletal hand was a fragment of parchment.

Fire*Wolf picked himself up and examined his surroundings more carefully. He was in a stone-lined pit. He was perhaps luckier than he deserved, for he saw it would be no great difficulty to climb back out again. The danger of the trap was the spike and he had missed that completely.

He glanced again at the skeleton, then, on impulse, prized the parchment fragment from its fingers. Although it was difficult to read in the half light, he eventually decided it must be a torn portion of a scroll. Part was written in an alphabet entirely unknown to him, the remainder in the common tongue of Harn.

What he could understand made little sense: it seemed to be part of some history or possibly some heroic myth.

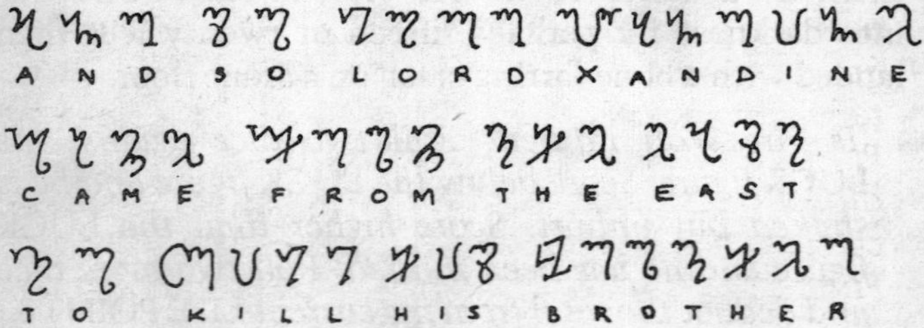

Frowning, Fire*Wolf tucked the fragment into his belt, then began to climb out of the pit.

*Fire*Wolf may, if he wishes and has the nerve, continue testing the levers at* **33**. *Alternatively, he may re-examine the situation from the perspective of* **27**.

46

'Very well!' Fire*Wolf growled. 'The bargain is struck.'

For an instant he felt a tiny flutter in his chest as if his heart had missed a beat, but nothing more.

At once the sword blade flared into blue-white light, illuminating the stone steps before him.

Without further hesitation, Fire*Wolf moved nimbly down them.

Move with him to **40**. *But first, permanently deduct three* LIFE POINTS *from his total. And remember that, from this point on, Fire*Wolf may use Doombringer as Lightbringer in situations of dark-*

*ness without further payment, thus avoiding the automatic first blow which would otherwise have gone to any creatures of darkness encountered. There is too an added bonus which you may like to note for subsequent combat encounters. If flared in an opponent's face, Doombringer will cause temporary blindness. To activate this option, Fire*Wolf must succeed in his first attempt at throwing a double dice roll to total less than his current* SKILL *figure. If the opponent is blinded, Fire*Wolf may strike three blows in succession without a return strike against him.*

47

In truth, there was not a great deal to discover.

Fire*Wolf soon concluded that while the leather-bound tomes might contain the inmost secret of the Universe, he, a simple Barbarian, was not equipped to decipher it. The runes and symbols of the magus who had once used this laboratory were far beyond his understanding.

Almost equally so were the retorts and vials on the shelves. Several of those which remained unbroken contained liquids or powders in varying colours. But the purpose of these compounds was beyond him. Did one swallow them? Or burn them? Or perhaps sprinkle them upon the ground while chanting mystic spells?

Quickly Fire*Wolf realized he was out of his depth. Yet the suspicion remained that some at least of the contents of this laboratory might prove useful to him. Thus, in desperation, he selected a small jar of sparkling blue powder for his experimentation. But what to do with it?

*What indeed? Shall he taste it? Go to **65**. Shall he set a light to it? Go to **75**. Shall he mix it with water? Go to **82**. Shall he throw some to the winds? Go to **90**.*

48

Fire*Wolf mounted the first tread of the spiral staircase at a run. For what had seemed to be a deserted castle, this one was proving far too dangerous for comfort.

His haste was a mistake. In a heart-stopping instant, the staircase spun on its own axis, gathering speed with a mechanical whine. Instinctively, he tried to jump off, but already it was too late. His surroundings blurred and the whine, growing higher and higher in pitch, seemed to invade his very brain. His senses reeled and carried him, still spinning, into darkness.

*An unpleasant surprise and one which might betoken sorcery at work. Where Fire*Wolf will end up now, lies in the lap of chance. Roll one die.*

Score		*Section*
1	*go to*	**43**
2	*go to*	**44**
3	*go to*	**51**
4	*go to*	**55**
5	*go to*	**59**
6	*go to*	**69**

49

Gingerly, Fire*Wolf pushed the first and third levers upwards, the second down. He waited.

After a moment, there was the grinding sound of machinery, causing him to jump back like a startled hare.

The sound stopped. Fire*Wolf waited a moment longer, then cautiously tried the door. It remained solidly locked.

Yet machinery had been set in motion.

He glanced around, but could find nothing changed. Then a small draught of air caused him to look upwards. A trap door had opened in the ceiling above his head.

*For Fire*Wolf, climbing to the trap door would be easy. But should he follow this route? If you decide that he should, turn to* **34**. *Alternatively, he has the options of continuing to experiment with the levers (***33***) or totally reconsidering his position from the perspective of* **27**.

50

Fire*Wolf prodded the prone corpse of the pantherine with his foot. It was a mature example of its species, a dangerous enemy and one seldom encountered alone since it was, by nature, a pack hunter. Perhaps the remainder of the pack were nearby . . .

The thought set Fire*Wolf's nape prickling.

Close by the pantherine's remains was the small sack in which these semi-sentient creatures carried their few crude belongings. Fire*Wolf flicked it open with the tip of his Doomsword and found to his delight a bundle of a dozen torches and a tinderbox, doubtless stolen from some less fortunate visitor.

In a moment he had one torch lighted and he poised, flamesword in one hand, torch held high in the other, eyes darting round the chamber in search of the pantherine pack.

And there, indeed, they were: black shadows, still as statues, a dozen or more ranged around the walls, watching him.

Rash Barbarian though he was, Fire*Wolf had no thought of tackling a full pantherine pack. Only death lay in that direction. Thus he moved slowly, eyes never leaving the savage beasts, towards the spiral staircase.

The pack stirred uneasily and several of its members snarled.

*A tense situation. To evaluate its outcome, throw two dice. Any score below 6 indicates the pack are likely to attack. But even so, Fire*Wolf may prove lucky. If the dice indicate an attack possibility, roll two dice more, multiplying the result by eight. If this final total is less than Fire*Wolf's* LUCK *figure, then the beasts will change their mind. If all else fails, our hero will have to fight. For convenience, assume twelve pantherines to the pack and assume too that each pantherine has the same stats as those listed for the one already killed. If Fire*Wolf is killed, go to* **13**. *If he manages to reach the staircase, go to* **48**.

51

Sorcery indeed! It was daylight and Fire*Wolf found himself confined in a narrow wooden cage hanging some fifteen feet above a courtyard. He was naked, but the Doomsword lay like an evil omen on the floor of the cage.

He was still in the castle. From his cramped vantage point he could see the looming, grey, deserted towers, the walls and beyond them the sullen lake and forest.

He examined the cage. It was constructed of stout boughs, lashed together with strong rope and suspended by a thicker rope from a high timber framework set close by the battlements. Below him, the courtyard seemed deserted.

Fire*Wolf picked up the Doomsword. At once its foul energy flowed through his veins.

'Where are we?' he asked brusquely.

'I fear I cannot say,' the suave voice echoed in his mind. 'I am aware of elapsed time, but it seems we have been spirited here by mystic arts. We remain somewhere in the castle, of course, but you know that already.'

'Can you cut through the bindings of this cage?'

'Of course.'

Thus, with the Doomsword, Fire*Wolf began carefully to cut through the ropes until he was able to remove three of the bars, a sufficient space for him to squeeze through. He slid, clung briefly by his fingertips, then dropped to the courtyard below. He landed badly, so that he was momentarily breathless, but no real damage was done. The Doomsword materialized on the stones beside his feet and he picked it up fatalistically. The castle was fraught with dangers: he had need of his terrible weapon.

The courtyard was small with only two exits – a

wooden gate to the east and a narrow doorway set into the northern wall.

*Which route should our hero take? You are Fire*Wolf. Choose the gate and go to* **66**. *Choose the door and go to* **76**.

52

The door collapsed with a crash as Fire*Wolf brushed against it. He was in a corridor, the walls of which were decorated with the remnants of ancient rotted tapestries. Cobwebs and dust were everywhere, as if this section of the castle had lain empty of intruders for many years. Nonetheless, he moved forward cautiously.

Those of the tapestries which had not completely faded told him little. One depicted a battle; another peasants harvesting grain. A third depicted the face of a beautiful woman, with the name 'Arcana' woven beneath it.

The corridor passed through an archway leading directly to a flight of steps downwards. Beside the archway was a wooden door.

And again the choice is yours. Through the wooden door will lead to **67**. *Down the steps and go to* **83**.

53

Fire*Wolf pulled the first and second levers downwards, hesitated breifly, then pushed the rightmost lever up.

He waited.

Nothing. Nothing happened. Return to **33** *and try again.*

54

Fire*Wolf edged forward, left hand on the wall to steady himself, feet carefully feeling for step after step. The sword remained in his right hand, ready for any emergency. His ears strained nervously to detect the slightest sound.

He counted fifteen steps in all before his feet discovered the bottom and the wall left him, suggesting he had entered a chamber. Cautiously he moved forward, already more than half regretting he had not taken up Doombringer's offer of light.

His caution was rewarded. A probing foot felt the edge of a drop. He moved to determine the outline and concluded he had reached an open pit, perhaps five foot square: a dangerous trap in the darkness.

Moving even more cautiously now, Fire*Wolf skirted the pit, left hand outstretched, still seeking the guidance of the wall. Almost immediately he reached a second pit. This he skirted too, moving even more slowly than before . . . and almost at once found himself on the edge of a third.

Still no indication of a wall for guidance. He edged his foot along, probing for a secure placement. As he did so, he heard the breathing.

Fire*Wolf spun round. Feral eyes glowed in the darkness. He had just time to raise his sword as the creature sprang.

55

Oh dear, oh dear! What an uncommonly difficult situation for our brave Barbarian. He is facing, though he does not know it (and cannot see it) a pantherine – one of the swiftest and most deadly predators in Harn. No supernatural creature this: merely a jet-black feline of high intelligence, rudimentary speech and vile disposition, in appearance like a cross between a panther and an ape. As always, you will find the creature's stats on page 248.

*But before you begin to calculate the outcome of this encounter, two points must be made. The first is that there is a small chance Fire*Wolf can avoid a fight. Compare the pantherine's* CHARM *figure with that of Fire*Wolf. If Fire*Wolf's figure is higher, then our Barbarian may be permitted one double dice roll, multiplied by eight, against his own* CHARM *figure. If he scores below that figure, then the pantherine will immediately abandon its attack, in which case you should turn to* **68**. *But should Fire*Wolf fail, the fight is on. In this event, each blow that Fire*Wolf strikes must be accompanied by a second roll of a single die. Unless he scores above 3 with this roll, you may take it he has fallen down a pit. Should he fall, go direct to* **42**. *Should the pantherine kill him, go to* **13**. *Should he kill the pantherine, go to* **50**.

55

He was on the battlements of the castle, in broad daylight, looking down on the sullen, mist-enshrouded lake. Almost immediately behind him a flight of stone steps led downwards into a small chamber. To his right towered the castle wall, devoid of doors but with one large, broken and unshuttered window through which he could certainly climb. He glanced through it into what appeared to be another chamber, deserted, empty except for a few sticks of broken furniture.

*Which route for Fire***Wolf? Down the steps and go to* **71**. *Through the window and go to* **84**.

56

Doomsword in hand, Fire*Wolf approached the door. As he did so, his keen ears heard a faint sound beyond it. He froze, waiting.

The sound was not repeated.

Fire*Wolf took a deep breath to still the pounding of his heart then reached out cautiously to try the handle of the door. Slowly, carefully, he turned it. Then, in a single swift movement, he jerked the door open.

A huge armoured figure fell upon him, so quickly he did not even have time to raise the Doomsword. Fire*Wolf tried to throw himself to one side, but succeeded only in losing his footing so that he fell heavily, with the weight of his attacker on top of him.

For an instant he lay winded, then began to fight . . . only to discover his weighty opponent lay still as stone.

Fire*Wolf extricated himself painfully.

The figure was not a warrior in armour, but a metallic representation of a man, crafted in brass, arms, legs and neck jointed to allow movement. A mechanical man? Fire*Wolf had no means of knowing, and in the

Wilderness Way, little interest. This creature could not harm him and that was all he wished to know. Beyond the door lay no more than a storage cupboard and in it, scampering startled from the crash, a mouse.

*Nothing more for Fire**Wolf *here. Return to* **43** *and reconsider his options.*

57

Fire*Wolf raised a silent prayer to his Wilderness gods. Some imp whispered that the move he was about to make would prove disastrous. Nonetheless he made it. One by one he pulled the levers downwards.

He waited.

Nothing. Nothing happened. Return to **33** *and try again.*

58

For an instant there was utter stillness, a nightmare tableau with no outcome possible other than Fire*Wolf's swift and sudden death.

The pantherines stirred uneasily, sniffing the air.

Fire*Wolf raised the lantern high, thinking to throw it towards the pack in the hope that burning oil might cut a path for him through the ring. Behind him, sensed rather than seen, the foul head of the first undead warrior emerged over the edge of the pit.

And the pantherines fled howling.

Fire*Wolf spun round to face this even more ghastly foe. The rotting corpses were crawling from the pit in large numbers now, halting to range themselves in a nightmare satire of military precision.

Skin crawling, instincts howling for flight like the pantherines, Fire*Wolf nonetheless prepared himself for his final battle.

And the growing Undead Army raised their arms to him in silent salute.

For a moment, Fire*Wolf remained rigid with shock. There was no mistaking the gesture of subservience. Or was there? Carefully he eased out of his crouched fighting posture. Again the Undead saluted, and again. One took a single pace forward. The tattered rags and rusted breastplate bore the faded remnants of a Sergeant-at-Arms insignia.

'Your orders, Commander!' the creature said.

Orders? Would these ghastly creatures really obey his orders?

'Go back!' ordered Fire*Wolf promptly.

At once the army turned and began to climb back into the pit.

'Stop!' shouted Fire*Wolf, his courage totally restored (and his curiosity greatly aroused, if the truth be known). 'Who are you?'

'We are the Castle Guard. We serve the Lord of the Valley.'

'But I am not – ' Fire*Wolf began, then stopped. Rash he might be, but never stupid. If these monsters had mistaken him for the Lord of the Valley, then it was scarcely in his best interests to disabuse them of the notion. He coughed, then called out with great confidence: 'Return whence you came, Castle Guard, and await my further orders!'

'At once, Lord,' the Undead Sergeant replied.

Before the last of them had disappeared, Fire*Wolf was running for the spiral staircase, casting a mental prayer of thanks to the Wilderness gods who had delivered him from the jaws of Hell.

Go to **48**.

59

For a moment Fire*Wolf was disoriented. It was daylight and he was no longer indoors. Of that he was certain. Yet the light was dim and there was a roof above his head.

Then the fog cleared from his mind and he realized he was staring upwards at sunlight filtering through the broad leaves of an overhanging tree. He stood up painfully, the Doomsword still clutched firmly in his hand, and looked around.

He was definitely outside the castle, although not far outside since he could see the towering walls no more than a dozen feet distant. He seemed to be in some sort of garden, long untended and now grossly overgrown. But how had he come here? He had no idea, although the fleeting thought of sorcery now loomed even larger in his mind.

Where to go? One direction seemed as good as any other.

But perhaps not. Go west, back towards the castle? Then go to **77**. *Or seize the opportunity of leaving the* *accursed place? East takes Fire*Wolf to* **85**, *south to* **91**, *north to* **96**.

60

He opened the door cautiously, Doomsword in hand. It led directly into a second chamber, smaller than the laboratory itself, square in shape and only dimly lit from a single high slit window.

Fire*Wolf hesitated. Even in the dim light he could see the outlines of a circle drawn upon the floor, mystic sigils around its circumference. Within the circle stood a rusted iron tripod supporting a shallow bowl of brass. The faint, sweet smell of ancient incense clung to the very stones. A magical workroom and Fire*Wolf's superstitious instinct warned him not to enter.

But should he heed his instinct? If you decide he should not, then go to **86**. *If you feel, with Fire*Wolf, that discretion might be the better part of valour, return to* **43** *and reconsider the options.*

61

Fire*Wolf reached out and pulled the first and third levers downwards.

Nothing happened.

With a faint shrug, he pushed the second lever upwards.

The ground dropped out beneath his feet.

Fire*Wolf experienced an instant of confusion as he fell into the pit, then the sharp agony of the vicious spike which impaled him. But the pain was mercifully short-lived.

Go to **13**.

62

Fire*Wolf stumbled, exhausted by the recent battle. He dropped on one knee and, throwing out a hand to steady himself, found himself touching a sack. This was, he realized instantly, the pantherine's carrier. The semi-sentient creatures often owned a few simple possessions which they collected together in sacks. He fumbled within, half hoping to find another weapon which would ease his reliance on the cursed Doomsword, and found instead something almost as useful – a bundle of torches and a tinderbox which the pantherine had obviously stolen from some earlier traveller.

In a moment, Fire*Wolf had a torch lit. He was, he found, in a large, circular chamber, its floor chequered in a series of open pits. A spiral staircase in metal lay beyond them.

But for the moment, neither the pits nor the staircase were his main concern. Ranged around the walls like demons from the deepest pit of Hell were twelve further pantherines. It was the main pack, one of whose number Fire*Wolf had already slaughtered.

To fight the entire pack, even with the Doomsword, was out of the question. To flee back the way he came was to become trapped in a dead end. Thus Fire*Wolf took the only possible course open to him. With no more than an instant's hesitation, he ran for the spiral staircase.

An understandable decision, but will he make it? Roll two dice to discover whether the pantherines *are disposed to attack. Score below 6 and they are. But even here, Fire*Wolf may escape with a whole skin. Throw two further dice, multiplying the result by eight. If your final total is less than Fire*Wolf's* LUCK *figure, then he will escape. Should it come to a battle, assume each pantherine's stats are identical to those of the single pantherine he has already killed and take each of the twelve encounters in sequence. Should Fire*Wolf be killed, go to* **13**. *Should he survive and escape, turn to* **48**.

63

Fire*Wolf opened the door, teetered on the threshold, then threw himself backwards only just in time. Before him was a sheer drop downwards to the dried-out moat. The door was set into the outer wall of the castle.

Cautiously, Fire*Wolf peered downwards, wondering at this strange and dangerous arrangement. On closer inspection he now noticed metal spikes set into the wall at intervals, forming rungs down which a man might climb. An ancient escape route, perhaps? But an escape route into what must once have been a full, deep moat. Hardly the best way to flee an enemy . . .

Except that the rungs did not continue all the way down. Less than four feet above the level of the moat they ended and though he could not be certain, he thought there was some sort of entrance to the castle set near the lowest of them. Yet, unless his eyes deceived him, this entrance was set just below what would have been the water level of the moat. An ancient secret entrance? Only climbing down the rungs would tell. But would the metal spikes still support weight? He would be in a precarious position indeed before he found the answer.

*Weighty considerations. Should Fire**Wolf *decide to climb down to explore, go to* **80**. *Otherwise return to* **43** *and reconsider his options.*

64

Arcana smiled slightly without rancour. 'As you wish, Barbarian.' She stood up. 'Now I must present greetings from the Lord of the Valley who requests the honour of your company if you feel strong enough to join him.'

'The Lord of the Valley?' Fire*Wolf echoed.

'My master, the Lord Xandine. He awaits your pleasure.'

So the castle was not deserted after all. Arcana and other women lived in it and now this Lord Xandine, whoever he might be. Despite appearances and the prowlers in the lower regions, it seemed the keep might house a retinue. Lord of the Valley? A sorcerer perchance, to judge from his demesne.

'I am not dressed to visit a great Lord,' Fire*Wolf murmured.

This time Arcana smiled broadly. 'You will find suitable garments in the chest beneath the bed.' She turned to the door. 'I shall await you outside.'

Fire*Wolf pulled the chest from beneath the bed and discovered fresh undergarments of linen and a long silken robe. It was a far cry from the raiment to which he was accustomed and he felt foolish as he dressed. But the robe fitted him to perfection. He walked from the room to find Arcana waiting in the corridor outside.

She glanced at him admiringly, but only said, 'Please follow me.'

And we too shall follow her . . . to **72**.

65

Fire*Wolf placed a grain or two of powder cautiously on the tip of his tongue. It tingled slightly, but otherwise produced no result.

He took a deep breath and swallowed almost a spoonful, then waited.

*A foolhardy action perhaps. Throw two dice and multiply the result by eight. Compare your final figure with Fire*Wolf's* LUCK *figure. If it is higher than his* LUCK *go to* **73**. If lower, go to **94**.

66

Fire*Wolf stepped through.

He had just enough time to register the fact that he was in another courtyard before a snarling shape launched itself towards his throat.

*No peace for our Barbarian. It would appear Fire*Wolf has been attacked by a greathound, one of the viciously trained hunting dogs so beloved of the sporting nobility of Harn. Worse still, a twin of the hound is even now approaching to mount a second attack. You will find the hounds' stats on page 248. The first beast will have first strike. The second, which attacks in sequence, will not. If Fire*Wolf survives go to* **74**. *If not, go to* **13**.

67

He was in a dining room of sorts. Not large, no banquet hall this, but a chamber in which one man and possibly a companion might take a meal in privacy, and comfort. Like so much of this accursed castle, the chamber had not been used for years. Thick dust lay everywhere.

There were two doors in the room apart from the one which he had opened and one of these two was small, set some three feet above floor level. Curiously, Fire*Wolf opened it to find himself looking down a narrow shaft. Twin ropes ran from a pulley downwards and though he had never seen such a device before, Fire*Wolf imagined it might be some form of server by which food was dispatched upwards from kitchens presumably below.

He turned his attention to the second door and found it securely locked – or perhaps simply jammed. For a moment he paused, undecided.

*Should he perhaps force the door? Fire*Wolf is strong and there are chairs here which he might use to break it down or indeed, Doombringer might splinter the wood. Alternatively, there is that shaft. Should he attempt to climb down it? If he attempts to force the door, go to* **78**. *If he decides to climb down the shaft, go to* **93**.

68

As the creature retreated, Fire*Wolf noticed the remainder of the pantherine pack – a dozen or so of the fierce creatures – ranged around the walls. But they too showed no indication that they were preparing to attack.

Cautiously he moved forward, his eyes never leaving the snarling creatures, until he reached the spiral staircase.

Go to **48**.

69

For a mind-wrenching moment he seemed suspended in space. Fragmentary visions flitted before his eyes, fleeting as dreams. Armies in battle. A great stone circle. A giant anarchid, larger than a greathound. An ancient on a granite throne, emaciated, pale and wrinkled as a corpse. A rock pool around which sported naked women.

Fire*Wolf fell in a slow spiral. As he fell it seemed that he was presented with a choice of two doorways, both ajar. Through one he could see the inviting form of a woman of breathtaking beauty. Through the other, a hand beckoned, an old hand, skeletal with parchment skin, on one finger of which was a huge, imposing seal ring.

*And his choice is real, although symbolic. If Fire*Wolf is attracted by the woman, go to* **44**. *Should the beckoning hand pique his curiosity, go to* **72**.

70

She smiled and reached up to the fastening of her robe.

In a moment the garment slid down to her feet. Beneath it, she was perfectly naked and perfectly formed. Fire*Wolf felt his passions rising as his eyes travelled across her body.

'Enjoy, Barbarian,' she murmured throatily as she slid beneath the sheet beside him.

Common decency might require us to draw a discreet veil over what will happen next, but all will be described in the fullest possible detail. Turn to **79**.

71

The steps were narrow and enclosed. Fire*Wolf moved cautiously. This castle had already thrown up too many surprises. It was well that he did, for on turning a corner in the stairwell, he found himself teetering on the edge of an open pit. Beyond it, the steps continued downwards.

The pit was not particularly wide – he could have jumped across it with little difficulty – but its position made it dangerous. He knelt to examine the edge more closely and found what he had expected: traces of an ancient cover and a tilt mechanism. At one time, this pit had been covered, a trap for the unwary.

He was about to rise when something caught his eye. In the pit, a short distance down, nearly invisible in the gloom, was a slim rope strung from one side to the other. A rope or a cable perhaps. It did not seem precisely like any other rope he had seen. Had someone once used the rope to escape from the trap? He could not tell, but he did know a rope might prove a singularly useful item to him.

By lying flat he could, he thought, just reach it. But as he began to do so, some subtle danger sense, bred of the Wilderness, caused him to hesitate.

*Should Fire*Wolf heed his instinct and leave the rope alone? Only you can say. If he chooses to take the rope, go to* **81**. *Should he abandon the attempt, go to* **87**.

72

Something was happening to Fire*Wolf's mind.

Without knowing how or why, he found himself walking in a dream. Events took on a fluid, shifting quality that was at once perfectly real and quite unreal. He felt no fear, no more than a marginal unease and walked forward bravely, his right hand hovering close to the hilt of the Doomsword.

Images flitted across the field of his perceptions like the ghosts of past events. A woman of great beauty who might, or might not, be walking at his side . . . Living corpses in a deep, wide pit . . . A prison chamber and a runic message . . . A sullen lake . . . Death and danger. . .

Were these things real? He did not know and found no means of knowing. Something was happening to his mind. He could only walk onwards, drawn by a sense of purpose that might, or might not, be connected with his destiny.

It seemed he reached a long, broad, high-ceilinged hall, colonnaded with granite pillars, slabbed with well-worn granite flagstones. The hall was at once empty and crowded. Shades of noble lords and ladies moved about their silent business, fading, disappearing, reappearing like the phantom manifestations of a will o'the wisp. Fire*Wolf heard distant conversation, distant laughter, distant music. . .

His mind cleared. There was total silence. The ghostly shades had disappeared, although the great hall remained. Fire*Wolf found himself dressed in a rich, full-length, silken robe, similar to those worn by the nobles he had seen. He was standing in the centre of the granite colonnades. And he was not alone.

The Lord of the Valley

Fire*Wolf stared along the sweep of the great grey pillars to an elevated granite throne. Upon it sat a solitary, hunched figure in the rich, dark robes of a practitioner of the Mystic Arts. The face was wrinkled like a wizened prune, the hand clutched on the armrest was little more than a skeletal claw. But the dark eyes, fastened on Fire*Wolf's own, glittered with fierce purpose and the voice, when the figure spoke, was strong.

'Approach me, Fire*Wolf!'

Fire*Wolf felt his legs move of their own volition as he walked reluctantly to the foot of the throne. He sensed menace in this wizened figure, or, if not menace, at least power. For the first time, he dearly wished the Doomsword was in his hand, but his arm remained immobile, as if paralysed. He reached the bottom step of the dais and stopped.

'I am the Lord Xandine,' the figure said without preamble. 'You see me in the process of dying.'

'Dying?' echoed Fire*Wolf in his mind, although his lips remained still.

'Aye, dying,' said the Lord Xandine, as if he had heard the thought. 'I have been engaged in dying for three centuries or more. It is a difficult task for one such as I, but my time has almost come. Thus I called you to me.'

'Called me?' This time Fire*Wolf spoke aloud.

The wizened figure sighed, as if the weight of ages rested on his shoulders. 'Your coming here was no accident.' The skeletal hand stirred, pointed, and

Fire*Wolf found himself staring at a chair which he could have sworn had not been there before. 'Please sit down, Fire*Wolf the Barbarian, and I shall tell you my story, for it will become of great importance to you.'

Cautiously, Fire*Wolf sat. The chair proved perfectly solid.

'I am called Xandine,' the figure said. 'It is not a name you will recognize. I was born far from this place, in a land beyond the mountains. My family is an ancient line of the Delai, a race which has long devoted itself to the exploration of strange paths of knowledge. I have a certain interest in sorcery myself, as you may have guessed from my attire.

'I was a noble among the Delai, not a ruler, but one of the aristocracy. The ruling House was called Harkaan. Between the Xandine and the Harkaan, there was sometimes friendship, sometimes enmity. At the time of which I speak, there was actual war – rebellion, you might say. The war was the instigation of the head of the House of Xandine, my elder brother, Darkwood. I was young then, disinterested in politics, but I was caught up in the conflict and fought my share of battles when I could not avoid them.

'The rebellion proved a disaster for my House. In its second year, the Xandine forces were routed and my brother forced into exile. He travelled across the mountains into Harn and eventually established this fortress in this valley.

'There the story might have ended, but Darkwood was ever ambitious and harboured dreams of returning to Kaandor, the land of the Delai, and toppling the House of Harkaan. He dispatched spies and even mounted the occasional sortie when the snows thawed in the mountain passes. He never after became a great danger to the Harkaan, but he was certainly a great nuisance. Furthermore, his activities created a focal point for various crackpot dissidents. Eventually he grew to be such an irritation that Harkaan again moved against the remnants of the Xandine in Kaandor.

'I was at the time the ruling Lord Xandine. The fortunes of my House were, of course, greatly depleted, but the Harkaan had recognized my fundamental disinterest in the early conflict and permitted me to retain certain of my estates.

'The Harkaan then moved brutally. They slew my wife and kidnapped my son, a baby boy then. They delivered an ultimatum that unless I put a stop to my exiled brother's activities, the child would be killed.'

The ancient figure sighed at the memory. 'I had little option. I crossed the passes into Harn, came to this valley and slew my brother. It was an act of great treachery, for he trusted me, but it was a necessity – or so I thought at the time. But the Harkaan did not release my child. They clearly thought of him as hostage to my own good behaviour now that Darkwood was dead. So, for the first time, I laid my own plans.

'I decided to put my lifelong interest in sorcery to good account. I had been a student only until then, but now I became a practitioner. First, I set up protection for my brother's former demesne, this valley, using a magical operation so potent, so dangerous that it had not been used for three thousand years. I placed a Time Lock on the valley. It meant that those within the Lock could not truly die while the magic endured. Intruders, by contrast, could die all too easily.

'Next, I worked to secure the safety of my child. This was even more difficult, since the boy was in the grasp of the Harkaan. Nonetheless, I was inspired to lay a subtle spell upon him so that even the Harkaan sorcerers believed him dead.

'They acted precisely as I had calculated. A substitute child was found in order to maintain the illusion of a hostage and the body, as they believed, of my true son was taken secretly from Kaandor and hidden in the Wilderness beyond Kaandor and Harn.

'But the boy was not, of course, truly dead. Aided by my craft, he was found by a tribe of Wilderness Barbarians and raised as one of their own. I was content to have it so, since he would, I knew, be safe in the Wilderness from any interference by the House of Harkaan.

'Meanwhile, I continued my subtle warfare against the royal house of Kaandor. For the most part, they did not even realize they were under attack. The finest among them fell prey to mysterious illnesses, curious accidents. Thus, gradually the dynasty weakened, and in weakening, began to lose control of Kaandor itself. Rebellions, revolts, internecine wars erupted with increasing frequency – and became more and more difficult to put down.

'For almost thirty years it has been so. In that single generation, I have brought the House of Harkaan almost to its knees. But now, in an attempt to unite the realm, the House has declared a new crusade into

Harn. Such crusades have been mounted in the past, with success and the present Lord Harkaan is convinced another may restore the fallen fortunes of his line. In this I fear he may well be correct, for an external enemy will always unite a people and the spoils of battle leave men at least temporarily content.'

For the first time, Fire*Wolf spoke. 'But why, "Venerable Ancient," do you not use your sorcery again in this matter?'

Lord Xandine actually smiled. 'The answer is contained in your very question. You call me 'Venerable Ancient', yet in truth I am no more than twenty-eight years older than yourself. What you see in my body, in this castle, in the valley itself, is the ravages of the Time lock. It is powerful sorcery and like all power exacts a fearful price. The Lock has almost run its course and for nearly a year now has been crumbling. Death is already possible within the valley and soon, for every creature here, death will be inevitable. The Lock absorbs our substance and makes monsters of us, each in our own way, before we perish completely.'

'So the House of Harkaan must triumph,' Fire*Wolf remarked.

'Perhaps not,' said Xandine. 'My war is almost over, that is true. But the new Lord Xandine may succeed where I have failed.'

'The new Lord Xandine?' Fire*Wolf asked. 'This son of whom you have spoken?'

The wizened figure moved painfully on the granite throne. 'You, Fire*Wolf,' he said. 'You are my son.'

*A shock indeed for our Barbarian. Fire*Wolf has always known he was not truly Wilderness born. But the son of a Kaandor noble? Can this really be true? Turn at once to* **88** for the outcome of this intriguing development.

73

The pains started almost instantly: a burning sensation in his throat, cramps in his stomach, a creeping weakness in his legs.

Once before he had felt like this when he had inadvertently eaten some poisonous fungus. But the virulence of his symptoms now were far greater than anything he had experienced before.

Desperately he tried to make himself sick, to rid his system of the toxin.

But to no avail.

*Hum the Death March for Fire*Wolf and go to* **13**.

74

Fire*Wolf stared down at the corpses of the greathounds and mentally calculated the extent of his own wounds. This castle, he now knew, despite the superficial appearance it gave of being deserted, was desperately dangerous. But were its inhabitants only beasts and monsters – or did someone (some*thing*) still rule here? More importantly, should he stay to find out, or attempt to discover an exit from the castle as quickly as possible?

He looked around. There was little of interest in this second courtyard except for kennels for the hounds.

Yet, on examination, he found fresh water left for the beasts in those kennels, suggesting that someone in this wretched place still looked after them.

Carefully Fire*Wolf searched for traces and was led to the only other exit from this second courtyard, a small doorway leading back into the main body of the castle itself. It opened easily enough and led into a short ground floor corridor. This he followed to a half-open door, which he pushed through cautiously to find himself in what must once have been the castle kitchens, although these were now patently disused.

Or were they? A side of fresh meat was hanging from a beam and a half-open sack showed palatable vegetables mixed in with others that were rotting. Yet jars and pots were broken, knives rusted and dust and cobwebs everywhere. There was a strange mystery here.

Two doors led out of the kitchens and what seemed to be a third proved, on inspection, to be the opening of a shaft running upwards to the floors above. From indications of broken machinery and a rotted rope, Fire*Wolf judged this might once have been a service shaft by which meals were sent up to the higher levels.

He was about to investigate the exit doors when a sound sent him whirling round, his hand dropping instinctively to the hilt of the Doomsword. Only feet away from him was an ancient crone, black eyes glittering in a deeply lined face, a rusted kitchen knife gripped like a dagger in her hand.

*What now, Fire*Wolf? Despite the knife, the old woman does not represent a serious threat perhaps. And although Fire*Wolf's previous attentions have* *concentrated on younger women of more comely mien, here may be an opportunity for him to try his* CHARM. *Throw two dice, multiplied by eight and compare the result against his* CHARM *figure. If the result is higher, go to* **89**. *If lower, go to* **95**.

75

Fire*Wolf sparked the tinder, then set the small flame to a conical heap of the blue powder poured on to the bench top.

At once he was dazzled by a flash so brilliant that it left him momentarily blinded.

When his eyes eventually recovered, he considered the situation thoughtfully. Without doubt had that flash occurred during combat, he would have been unable to strike a blow for two rounds. Thus the powder might, in certain circumstances, serve him as a weapon. He estimated that he had enough for a dozen such flashes in the jar.

*So Fire*Wolf has added a further weapon to his slow-growing armury, but one usable only in situations where there is an open flame into which he can throw the powder. Still, better than nothing. Return now to* **47** *so that he can reconsider his various options.*

76

Fire*Wolf tried the door and found it opened easily. He listened, but there was no sound. He stepped inside and found himself in what must have been the castle kitchens at one time, although now there was every indication of disuse.

Or was there? A side of fresh meat was hanging from a beam and a half-open sack showed palatable vegetables mixed in with others that were rotting. Yet jars and pots were broken, knives rusted and dust and cobwebs everywhere. There was a mystery here and Fire*Wolf felt uncomfortable with it.

Two doors led out of the kitchens and what seemed to be a third proved, on inspection, to be the opening of a shaft running upwards to the floors above. From indications of broken machinery and a rotted rope, Fire*Wolf judged this might once have been a service shaft by which meals were sent up to the higher levels.

He was about to investigate the exit doors when a sound sent him whirling round, his hand dropping instinctively to the hilt of the Doomsword. Only feet away from him was an ancient crone, black eyes glittering in a deeply lined face, a rusted kitchen knife gripped like a dagger in her hand.

*What now, Fire*Wolf? Despite the knife, the old woman does not represent a serious threat perhaps. And although Fire*Wolf's previous attentions have concentrated on younger women of more comely mien, here may be an opportunity for him to try his* CHARM. *Throw two dice, multiplyed by eight and compare the result against his* CHARM *figure. If the result is higher, go to* **89**. *If lower, go to* **95**.

77

Fire*Wolf entered the castle with a feeling of foreboding. Too many things about this place were proving beyond his immediate control. The Barbarian nature craved simplicity – enemies he could see, hear and fight with strong arm and trusty sword. The smell of sorcery nauseated him, and the smell of sorcery was everywhere in this place.

He passed into a narrow corridor, dusty and deserted as any in the castle, leading the Wilderness gods knew where. The doorway to the garden closed behind him, apparently of its own accord. He turned at the sound, but decided investigation would be a waste of time. Doors here closed of their own accord and while the mechanics of their action might be of interest to a wizard, there was nothing to be learned by a fighting man.

He turned back and found himself facing a green-eyed woman in a long white robe. In a moment of curious lucidity, he noticed she had left no traces of her approach in the dust on the corridor floor.

Fire*Wolf stopped. 'I offer you no injury, My Lady,' he said cautiously. Was she real? Was she flesh and blood? Or was she a spirit only, who flitted through these corridors without so much as disturbing the dust on the floors?

'Nor I you, Barbarian,' the woman said softly. She smiled a secret smile. 'Although we may perhaps offer one another some amusement.'

Amusement? Was there no sanity in this whole valley? None to be sure in this gloomy keep.

The woman gestured and a section of the wall slid back to reveal a secret doorway. Beyond was a room, a bedroom ablaze with candelabra and well-trimmed lamps. 'My quarters,' she said. 'Will you enter?'

'Who are you?' Fire*Wolf asked.

'I am called Yveen. And you, perchance, are Fire*Wolf?'

'You know my name?'

'I know your name, Barbarian.' She moved lightly into the room and fumbled with the fastening of her robe. 'We are destined to be allies, you and I.' The robe fell away to the waist, revealing her breasts. 'And lovers,' she added, smiling.

Fire*Wolf stared hungrily, primitive urges arising strongly to cloud his judgement. 'Allies?' he echoed. Then, more softly, 'Lovers?'

She turned and sat upon the bed, alluring in her sensual pose but making no attempt to remove her robe completely. At Fire*Wolf's side, the Doomsword hummed softly.

'Your sword knows me even if you do not. We are two of a kind, your blade and I. I tell you frankly, Fire*Wolf, I am no mortal woman.'

She looked a mortal woman. All too mortal and all too woman. Fire*Wolf moved clumsily towards her, his mind a maelstrom of confusion. 'Who are you?'

'My name you know,' she smiled. 'As to what I am, that is perhaps a more important question.' The green eyes glinted. 'You might call me a demon.'

Fire*Wolf's hand dropped to his sword, which seemed to rise to meet it, the gentle humming increased to a howl. 'Demon!' Fire*Wolf hissed.

She seemed more amused than frightened. 'Your sword hungers for me even if you do not, Barbarian. But before you take precipitate action, should you not first listen to what I have to say?'

*Perhaps. Perhaps not. Fire*Wolf is no sophisticate. As a man of action he is as likely to strike as to listen. If he strikes with the Doomsword, go to* **92**. *If he decides to listen, go to* **97**.

78

The lock was old but sturdy. The door itself was, perhaps, more infirm. Fire*Wolf drew back a pace or two, then flung his entire weight against it.

The door crashed inwards. Carried by his momentum, Fire*Wolf followed . . .

He plunged downwards in a shaft which carried him directly to a stony doom in caverns deep beneath the bowels of the keep.

Go to **13**.

79

Distracted by the slim hand caressing him and the soft warmth of the woman's body pressed so closely to his own, Fire*Wolf failed to notice the curious development of Arcana's teeth as she leaned with every indication of passion to kiss him on the throat.

But whether or not he noticed, the kiss was immediately transformed to nightmare. There was surprisingly little pain; only the warm gush of his life blood as the jugular was severed.

*There may be a moral here for Fire*Wolf. As he seeks it, turn to* **13**.

80

After only a moment's hesitation, Fire*Wolf swung himself down on to the first of the metal spikes. But he did not release his hand grip until he had thoroughly tested the effect of applying his full weight. The first spike held; as did the spike beyond.

Like a human fly he crawled slowly, spike by spike, down the castle wall.

But will he make the bottom safely? Add his current SKILL *figure to his* LUCK. *Now roll three dice and multiply the result by eight. If the final figure is less than the combined* SKILL/LUCK *total, go to* **98**. *If not, face the bad news right away: he falls – go to* **13**.

81

On his second attempt he gripped the rope.

And found his hand stuck fast!

The rope jerked violently, toppling him forward into the pit. At once he became aware of further ropes criss-crossing the trap and these too stuck fast to his body.

Fire*Wolf twisted in sudden terror. He could feel vibrations in the ropes as if something was moving along them from the depths towards him . . . and moving quickly. He thought he could see two glowing eyes in the darkness beneath. Furiously, he bent every effort towards freeing himself from the confining cables.

*And while Fire***Wolf will bend every ounce of strength to that vital task, we must ask ourselves if his strength is sufficient. Throw three dice, multiply by eight and compare the result with his* STRENGTH *figure. If lower, go to* **99**. *If higher, go to* **110**.

82

Fire*Wolf mixed the blue powder carefully with water and looked at it frowning. What, he wondered, had he created?

He had, in fact, created ink. It is of questionable benefit to a fighting man. Perhaps you should return to **47** *and reconsider his options.*

83

Fire*Wolf stepped through the archway and found himself falling. The steps, apparently so solid, proved as intangible as moonbeams. He fell through them, tumbling into darkness as if he had stepped voluntarily into an open pit.

For all he could do about it, he might have fallen to his death. But, twisting like a cat, he managed to land on his feet after no more than fifteen feet or so. It was a jar, but no damage was done.

He looked around.

He was in a stone-lined cell, a dungeon lit by the smoking flame of a single torch stuck askew in a wall-mounted bracket. The floor beneath his feet was damp and moisture streamed down the walls. One door led from this cell, stoutly made from oak and bound in metal. Hanging in chains from brackets on the wall opposite the door was the corpse of a half-naked, emaciated, bearded man.

The dampness struck Fire*Wolf as peculiar. Almost everywhere else in this accursed castle had been bone dry. It was as if he had dropped below the level of the lake; yet he could not have fallen far enough to have done so.

He looked up. The ceiling above his head was made of stone slabs and appeared solid. Yet he had fallen through it. And had not the stairs seemed solid as he passed through the archway? Fire*Wolf drew the Doomsword and hurled it upwards. The blade struck the ceiling with a clang before dropping back to his feet. The ceiling was solid all right . . . yet he had fallen through it. More sorcery afoot!

He moved to the door. It was, as he suspected, securely locked. Nor did the door itself seem likely to fall to any attack he might mount upon it with his limited equipment. As he was examining the door, he noticed a grid scratched into the wall immediately beside it. Cut into the grid were the following sequence of numbers.

2 9 1 4 8 7 6 5 3 9 4 6 7 8 8 3 1 2 3 4 5
6 7 8 9 8 7 6 5 4 3 7 9 8 7 6 5 4 3 2 1 9
8 7 6 5 4 3 2 1 2 1 6 2 1 7 2 8 9 1 2 1 2
3 4 5 6 7 8 9 1 2 3 4 5 6 7 1 5 2 1 6 3 1
7 4 6 1 3 5 1 2 4

Fire*Wolf stared at them uncomprehendingly. Although faded, they had obviously been put there for a purpose. He was still puzzling their significance when a weak voice behind him caused him to whirl around, reaching for his sword.

'They indicate the way out of here,' the voice said. It emanated from the emaciated prisoner hanging from the wall.

Fire*Wolf relaxed. 'My pardon,' he said grimly. 'I had thought you dead.'

'You thought correctly,' the prisoner said. 'My heart has ceased to beat. My vital functions have failed. But it is difficult to die in this accursed place, as you too may have discovered.'

Fire*Wolf, who had discovered nothing of the sort, remained silent.

'I remain here in the undead state until the magic that protects this valley is removed, or fades in time as it is fading now. Lord Xandine cannot last much longer and when he dies, his wizardry dies with him and I shall obtain release. Unless, of course, you release me sooner.'

'Assuredly I shall,' Fire*Wolf said, moving forward to examine the fetters. He did not in truth believe the man dead, merely demented by his sufferings.

But the bearded prisoner shook his head. 'To release me from my chains will not release me from my burden. I am Xandine's prisoner by reason of his magic rather than his fetters. To help me, you must hurry Xandine to his own fate, or perish in the attempt.'

'But I know no Lord Xandine,' Fire*Wolf protested, although the name did, in fact, tickle memory traces at the edge of his mind.

'Nonetheless, you are fated to meet him. Perhaps. But first you must leave this cell. In this, if in nothing else,

I can help you. Cut in the wall beside the door is an ancient tablet of Pythagorean number magic. Do you know numerals, Barbarian?'

Was he really talking to a corpse? 'I know them, but I have little skill with them,' Fire*Wolf admitted.

'Of that we shall soon discover. Examine the tablet and discover how many adjacent numbers add to ten. Then, when you have found the total, knock that number of times on the door. If you are correct, the door will open. If not, the sluices will be released and you will drown.'

'We will drown,' Fire*Wolf murmured.

'I do not breathe, I shall not drown. This cell is deep beneath the lake. There is only the escape by numbers.'

'How did I get here?'

'You were magically transported. There are many areas of the castle which will transport the unwary into situations such as this.'

Uncertainly, Fire*Wolf turned back to the door and its faded, engraved tablet.

*A simple task, one would imagine. But how many times will Fire*Wolf knock? If 7 go to* **100**. *If 8, go to* **111**. *If 9, go to* **119**.

84

A little wary of the broken shuttering, Fire*Wolf climbed through. There was little more to see now than when he had looked through the window from outside, save for one thing: from this vantage point he now saw there was a door leading from the room.

Fire*Wolf started towards it. The wooden flooring collapsed beneath his feet!

This is no small thing for our hero. It may, in fact, quite easily kill him. Throw two dice. Multiply the result by eight and compare it with his LUCK *figure. If the* LUCK *figure is higher, go to* **101**. *If not, it's the dreaded* **13**.

85

His decision made, Fire*Wolf moved eastwards, a sudden surge of relief in his breast that he was leaving the accursed castle, perhaps – with luck – leaving this whole accursed valley.

The garden was walled: that he knew. But he had no doubt he could scale the barrier. He moved more swiftly now, as his resolve grew.

Something wrapped itself around his ankle.

Fire*Wolf stopped just in time to prevent himself tripping. His foot, he saw, had become entangled in a thick creeper of a species he did not immediately recognize, but one which he now noticed was growing in some profusion in this area of the garden.

He leaned down to untangle his foot and a creeper curled round his wrist.

Fire*Wolf tried to jerk his wrist free and found he could not. The ground tangle of creepers writhed, moving slowly towards him like the slow tide of a sullen sea. With his free hand he reached desperately for the

Doomsword, but before he could draw it, another creeper wrapped around his entire body, pinning his arms. Fire*Wolf exerted his entire strength.

But to no avail . . .

A wrong decision. Go to **13**.

86

With his deepest instincts screaming silent alarms, Fire*Wolf stepped into the chamber.

Nothing happened.

Carefully skirting the circle, he examined the room. There was no door other than that by which he had entered. The high slit window was too narrow to climb through even if he reached it.

After a moment he knew there was nothing of value here. Yet still his instincts warned him of dire peril. He turned to leave, perhaps too hastily, and in his haste stumbled, dropping on one knee within the circle.

The creature that launched itself upon him materialized from thin air perhaps three feet above the floor, a faintly man-like shape as black as hell with fiery eyes and an all-pervasive smell of brimstone.

It was not particularly large – much smaller certainly than Fire*Wolf himself – but it was surrounded by an aura of such pure evil that his soul chilled.

The creature hissed.

Fire*Wolf twisted to avoid the charge and drew the Doomsword.

*Not pleasant. The entity disturbed by Fire*Wolf is a Demon. One of the lesser denizens of Hell to be sure, but intensely dangerous for all that. Turn to page 248 for the thing's stats. If Fire*Wolf survives, turn to* **102**. *If not, go to* **13**.

87

Fire*Wolf made the jump easily, landing with no more than a momentary imbalance at the other side of the pit.

He followed the narrow stairway downwards until he reached a blank wall.

He stopped, momentarily nonplussed, then considered that no one in their right mind would build a staircase which led nowhere. There had to be a door in the wall, a secret panel of some description. It could not be too difficult to find, for the stairway was obviously an escape route to the battlements rather than the other way around.

His questing fingers searched the wall, feeling for a crack, an indentation, anything that might give him the secret of the door.

Suddenly he found it! A loose stone which, when he worked it free, revealed a small ring set into the masonry. Fire*Wolf gripped it firmly and pulled.

With a grinding of stone on stone a section of the wall moved out towards him . . . and at the same instant he felt a sting in the palm of his hand.

Fire*Wolf snatched his hand away from the ring. A tiny spot of blood, no larger than a pinhead, had welled up from his palm. He stared at it in the half-light, wondering. It was nothing. Nothing at all.

The thought seemed to echo in his brain. It was growing darker. Darker and darker. Fire*Wolf moved forward on legs which had all but turned to marrow. His head swam, spun, then he fell forward heavily into the blackest darkness he had ever known.

Go to **44**.

88

'I?' Fire*Wolf echoed. He was stunned by the news, yet somehow did not think to question it. He knew, after all, that he was not Wilderness born. And this ancient had no reason to lie.

The hooded figure nodded. 'You are my son. Fate decreed that we should be separate, one from another, throughout most of your life and now that we have met, Fate decrees that we must soon part, for as I told you, I am dying. Thus I expect nothing from you, neither love nor affection nor any of the emotions that our relationship might have brought. But this I do say: the Xandine blood flows through your veins. That you cannot avoid. It is the blood of a sorcerous race, so mayhap you have a talent for sorcery you do not suspect . . .'

'No!' Fire*Wolf cried in horror. He had a dread of sorcery.

Lord Xandine shrugged. 'Perhaps not. It is of little import. But I have stared into the currents of Time and Space and while no amount of sorcery can part the mists completely, this I tell you. Your Fate and mine are inseparably interlinked. You are Delai by blood and Xandine by line. On my death you will become the new Lord Xandine. That I know. What you do as Lord Xandine is your own choice and decision. But it is a decision I will seek to influence in the small time that is left to me.'

Fire*Wolf stood dumb. The dreamlike quality of the moment had not left him. Was he really here, in this colonnaded hall? Or was this whole experience drug magic? Had the woman somehow fed him plants that would create a waking dream?

The ancient figure sighed. 'Naturally it is my hope that you will continue my war against the Harkaan, that you will avenge the wrong done by that House to your own. But it is my hope only. I would not force you even if it were still within my power. There is, however, one matter of which I have not yet told you. It may persuade you to tread the road I seek for you. That is the matter of the Demon-spawn.'

Something in Xandine's tone, or in the word itself, made Fire*Wolf's skin crawl. He waited.

'In this castle,' Xandine said, 'if you search it thoroughly, you will find a laboratory. Built off that laboratory is an oratory. Although the crumbling of the Time lock must by now have given both the appearance of long disuse, you may still discern a circle drawn on the oratory floor. Within that circle there is presently trapped an entity from the nether planes of Hell itself. It is a fearsome creature, called up by myself in the course of a sorcerous operation. But at least its powers are limited on this plane.

'In Kaandor, men of the Delai race have long communicated with entities such as this. More than seven thousand years ago, according to our written records, a Lodge of Sorcerers, allied to the denizens of Hell, created a new race of beings which partook of the characteristics of both planes – the Infernal and the Physical. This race, this artificial creation, proved intensely dangerous to humanity. Because of their origin, the race became known as the Demonspawn and the scriptures of the Delai show that for eight hundred years they were a pestilence in the land where they were created.

'It might have been that the Demonspawn would have subdued the Delai totally. The Spawn were by comparison few in number – they do not breed like natural stock, but work to create others of their kind by blood magic and it is a slow process. But few or not, they were virtually invincible and thus their power grew.'

The glittering orbs in the wizened face misted as if Xandine stared directly into the distant past of his own tale. 'Then there appeared among the Delai a woman of great power. Her name was Selina of the Lance and Orb – two mystic weapons of which she made much use. It is said she was no mortal woman but a goddess. Perhaps she was. Certainly she bound the Demonspawn, confining them to caverns in the frozen mountains dividing Kaandor and Harn. Having saved humanity from this curse, she disappeared.

'Matters of magic are never simple, Fire*Wolf. The structure of Time itself ensures that nothing may be considered absolute, nothing permanent. Thus, though the Spawn were confined and remain confined to this day by the ancient power of the Lance and the Orb, there have been periods when small numbers of them managed to release themselves to wreak havoc in the upper land. Sometimes they attacked Kaandor, sometimes Harn. Always they have been halted, because their numbers were few, but at fearsome cost. There is no doubt in my mind that should the day ever come when all the Demonspawn were loosed, that day would spell the destruction of humanity.'

He leaned forward on the granite throne. 'That day draws near, I fear.'

Fire*Wolf's head jerked up, his gaze locked on the eyes of his father. 'Say on.'

'I spoke of a crusade – a crusade to be mounted by the present head of the House of Harkaan. My Arts have told me something of his plans. In this crusade he seeks to ally himself with the Demonspawn, thinking to make use of them until his objective is achieved, then to confine them again as before. In this he is mistaken. Once loosed, the Spawn will turn against him.'

'Should you not rejoice at this?' asked Fire*Wolf sourly. 'It will mean the end of the Harkaan.'

'It will,' the ancient figure nodded. 'But the end too of all the Delai and of all humanity in Harn and in the lands beyond. There will be no Goddess Selina to rescue our breed a second time. The Spawn must be stopped and since the Spawn *cannot* be stopped, then the plans of the House of Harkaan must be thwarted before the Spawn are released. There is little time and I am dying. Thus I called you.'

For a moment, Fire*Wolf remained silent, speechless. Then he said, 'You want me to stop Lord Harkaan?'

Lord Xandine, the wizened sorcerer who claimed to be his father, nodded.

*Yet another decision for Fire*Wolf – and surely the most fateful of his life. But not a simple decision. For he has no means of measuring the truth of the words of this hooded wizard. And further, he is already under obligation to find and rescue Baldar's daughter. What then can he say? What will he say? If he agrees, turn to* **103**. *If he refuses, turn to* **112**.

89

With a feline hiss, the crone launched herself upon him.

Unwilling to injure one so obviously old and frail, Fire*Wolf abandoned his grip on the Doomsword and instead sought to reach her wrist and turn the knife thrust.

To his intense amazement, he discovered there was more strength in her arm than he would ever have believed possible. In the instant of realization, the knife poised momentarily above his heart.

*An unexpected peril. Compare Fire*Wolf's* STRENGTH *figure with that given for the old woman on page 249. If Fire*Wolf's figure is higher, go to* **95**. *If lower, go to* **104**.

90

And nothing happened.

After a moment, feeling foolish, Fire*Wolf set to reconsidering his options.

Return to **47** *to help him do so.*

91

Perhaps at some unconscious level the vista had influenced his choice. For here, the abandoned garden retained some of its former glory. His footsteps led him to a bank of wild orchids, flowering and thriving despite the season.

As he approached, he became aware of the scent, an alluring, musky fragrance which seemed to insinuate itself into his mind as much as his nostrils. He stopped, breathing in the beauty, and felt a strange tremor in his body.

The scent and his feelings strengthened and to his utter astonishment, he was suddenly aware of a strong but pleasurable sensation in his body.

Fire*Wolf walked close to the flowers, felt his feet carry him among them. As he did so, the feelings of pleasure in him strengthened more and more.

Trembling, Fire*Wolf lay down on the welcoming earth, his mind a turmoil, but his body quite unable to resist the cloying perfume that was everywhere. Again and again he found himself aware of strange sensations until numbness and exhaustion crept with dreadful inevitability throughout his limbs.

*What a way to go – but go he must. No sorcery this, however it might seem. Fire*Wolf has instead stumbled on a cultivation of the rare Passion*

*Orchid, a plant which ensures the fertility of its soil by the pleasurable entrapment of organic life which dies in ecstasy then rots to provide manure. There is no escape. Fire*Wolf is strong and well versed in the arts of love, yet no man can endure the intensity of these feelings for an indefinite time. We must go now to await him at* **13**.

92

The Doomsword howled from its sheath and cut a powerful arc through the air with such ferocity that it might have been facing the Arch Fiend himself.

A brilliant blue flash erupted as it struck Yveen. Fire*Wolf had just time to see the woman's figure disappear before the surge of energy flowed from the sword into his arm and erupted through every fibre of his body.

It erupted with too much force for mortal bones to bear. Go to **13**.

93

The shaft was cramped for one of Fire*Wolf's frame, but it enabled him to make good progress by bracing his back against one wall and his feet against the other.

It was difficult to judge distance travelling in this manner and moving in almost total darkness. But it seemed he must have traversed at least two levels downwards when the brickwork at his back abruptly crumbled.

In the instant of danger, Fire*Wolf's mind worked with such lightning speed that it seemed Time itself halted briefly. He knew he must fall to his death, yet there was one slim chance that he might push so strongly with his powerful legs as to break completely through the wall behind him.

An outside chance indeed, but the only one our hero has. Roll two dice and multiply the result by 24. Compare your final figure with the total of Fire∗Wolf's SPEED, STRENGTH *and current* SKILL *figures combined. If Fire∗Wolf's total is less than your result, go to* **13**. *If higher, go to* **113**.

94

Power coursed through Fire∗Wolf's sinews like a flame. A blue glow erupted from the hand which held the remaining powder, consuming it to ashes. But as the powder burned, the sensation of energy in Fire∗Wolf's body actually increased. He felt good.

As well he might. The action of the powder is twofold. It will bring him up to his full LIFE POINTS *should he be under that total at the moment and give him a reserve of 10* LIFE POINTS *in his next combat. Furthermore, two points are automatically added to his* SKILL. *A lucky find for Fire∗Wolf. Go now to* **43** *and decide what he will do next.*

95

The knife clattered on the stone floor and the ancient crone faced him placidly. 'What do you want of me?' she asked.

'I mean you no harm,' Fire∗Wolf hastened to reassure her. 'I seek only a safe way out of this accursed castle.'

The old woman shook her head. 'There is no safe way save at the pleasure of the Lord.'

'The Lord? This castle has a living Lord?'

'Living?' The old woman cackled abruptly. 'That's a matter of opinion. But a Lord nonetheless – Lord Xandine.'

'Can you take me to him?' asked Fire*Wolf eagerly.

'Aye, if you trust me. For to meet Lord Xandine I must first render you helpless.'

*Allow himself to be rendered helpless? That is surely something foreign to Fire*Wolf's independent nature. Yet the prospect of meeting the ruler of the castle is certainly tempting. If Fire*Wolf agrees, go to* **72**. *If not, turn to* **114**.

96

He grew cold. For a moment he thought he must be imagining the sensation, but the chill seemed to rise from the very earth itself. He hesitated, stopped. The cold was leeching into his very bones.

Locked in momentary indecision, Fire*Wolf half turned. His feet seemed rooted to the ground.

It was cold. So very cold.

And the earth was stealing the living warmth of his body . . .

A vortex of negative power, no doubt, such as are sometimes found in the land of Harn. Such places are always dammed when they appear in a garden or anywhere else that humans might frequent. But *not this one. Or perhaps the usual protections have broken down. The answer, in any case, has little relevance to Fire*Wolf. He is now well on his way to* **13**.

97

'Very well,' Fire*Wolf said. 'If listen I must, then listen I shall.'

The green eyes locked on his own. 'You might call me a demon, though that is not my true nature. Few things are exactly as they seem in Xandine's castle. It is my nature to test visitors to this place – and in the testing, many have been found wanting. Those who fail, die. Those who do not . . . well, that is another story.'

'And you propose to test me?'

'I have already tested you,' the woman said. 'You show self-control and forbearance. They are the prerequisites of a successful sorcerer.'

'Sorcerer?' Fire*Wolf snorted. 'I know naught of sorcery, nor want to.'

'Perhaps,' Yveen smiled. 'But if you will not meddle with sorcery, it may be your destiny that sorcery will meddle with you.' Abruptly, she extended her hand. 'The Lord of the castle wishes to meet with you, Barbarian.'

The Lord of the castle? 'Who is this Lord?' Fire*Wolf asked suspiciously.

'Why, Lord Xandine,' said the woman. Her hand remained outstretched. 'Will you come?'

*Well, will he? If Fire*Wolf is prepared to go meekly with this strange, beautiful woman who may – or may not – be a demon, go to* **72**. *If not, turn to* **105**.

98

With a feeling of relief he swung his body into the cramped, dark hole of the secret entrance.

He was in a tunnel, the walls of which were still slimed with dampness. It was too low to permit him to stand upright, but he moved forward, half crouched, his hand always hovering near the hilt of the Doomsword.

After perhaps fifteen feet, he met a solid barrier.

*Predictably enough, perhaps. If the entrance was originally below the level of the moat, then something had to stop the water getting in. But how will Fire*Wolf get past it? He might search for a hidden lever or some such device, in which case go to* **106**. *Or he might try to break his way through by main force since much of the castle is old and crumbling. If so go to* **115**.

99

With an almost superhuman effort, Fire*Wolf freed his arm. Using the Doomsword with desperate ferocity, he hacked wildly at the looming monster which was now almost upon him.

He had a brief glimpse of hirsute legs, fiery eyes, faceted like those of a gigantic insect, fangs dripping venom. . .

Then he was fighting for his very life.

Big is not always beautiful, it seems. Despite the gloom, Fire∗Wolf knows full well what he is facing: a spider so immense it could digest a carthorse (or a Barbarian) for breakfast. Which is, it would appear, precisely what the monster is proposing to do. Will Fire∗Wolf survive? There is only one way to find out. The spider's stats are listed on Page 249. If Fire∗Wolf wins the fight, go to **87**. *If not, there is nothing for it but the dreaded* **13**.

100

He hesitated, waiting.

There was a momentous silence that stretched into an eternity. Behind him he thought he heard the smallest groan from the shackled prisoner. Then, with a roar like thunder, water cascaded into the subterranean chamber. The force flung Fire∗Wolf from his feet and within seconds he was chilled to the bone in a fierce, swirling torrent. He clawed his way to the surface, lungs bursting with the effort. But that surface was rising with an awesome inevitability. . .

Put Fire∗Wolf out of his misery. Go to **13**.

101

For a moment he lay stunned amid the debris. As he tried to move, he discovered even the smallest effort sent wracks of pain throughout his body.

(Although he has survived the fall, he has not survived it unscathed. Half his current LIFE

POINTS *are now gone.)*

Eventually, however, he summoned sufficient resources to look around him. He seemed to be in a small, disused chamber – its only exit the gaping hole in the ceiling above his head.

*What now? Fire*Wolf might, of course, climb back and return the way he came. If so, go to* **55**, *which places him again on the battlements. Or he might search for a secret door . . . in which case go to* **107**.

102

The creature should be dead, but it was not. Although the Doomsword had absorbed every trace of life, it remained with horrible solidity before him. But now, at least, it did not attack. Instead, it bowed.

'You did well, puny human,' it remarked without a trace of rancour. 'For yourself and for me. By absorbing the life energies which held me here, you have permitted me release to my own Plane. It is the Law of my species that I must render you a service in return. What is it you wish?'

Fire*Wolf stared at the demon in blank revulsion, panting from the exertion of the fight and scarcely able to speak. A service? From this monster? All he really wanted was to be rid of it. The thing was a creature of sorcery and Fire*Wolf abhorred sorcery above all things. He said nothing.

The demon appeared to shrug. 'Very well. Your silence indicates you do not wish anything from me now. Nonetheless, the Law of my species exists and I cannot gainsay it. I am bound to you, Barbarian, until such time as you require my service and in requiring it, release me. Remember my name, which is Hamiel Achondrite. You need only call that name and I shall appear to aid you. But once only. And now, until you summon me – farewell.'

As Fire*Wolf watched, the ghastly form paled, grew translucent, then transparent before fading altogether. He shuddered. It would be a dire extremity before he evoked the aid of such a hellish creature.

*Be that as it may, it is as well to know exactly what Fire*Wolf has earned here by defeating and releasing the demon. He is owed one service and one only by the infernal creature. If evoked in combat, Hamiel Achondrite will appear to fight at Fire*Wolf's side, having identical* LIFE POINTS *to those shown on Page 248. If evoked outside of combat, the demon will carry Fire*Wolf back to any Section he has previously visited, with a full restoration of our hero's* LIFE POINTS *in the process.*

103

After an eternity of hesitation, Fire*Wolf bowed his head. He felt as though circumstances were taking his decisions for him as if he had somehow, mysteriously, been manipulated from childhood to reach this spot at this time. Was Xandine his father? He could scarcely deny it, for why would the wizard make such a claim if it were untrue? And if he were his father, then Fire*Wolf was bound to him by destiny of blood. There was no denying that either. More to the point, if what the failing Lord Xandine said about the Demonspawn was correct, then no other possible course of action was open – for what was more important than the salvation of humanity itself?

Nonetheless, Fire*Wolf remained troubled. He had still given his word to the hermit who had saved his life and whatever his bloodline, the Wilderness upbringing had made him a man of his word.

He raised his head and stared directly into his father's glittering eyes. 'One thing,' he said firmly. 'I have embarked upon a task from which I may not turn aside, for I am committed to a friend for its execution. If I am to fight the Harkaan, it must be after I have discharged my first responsibility.'

'The Harkaan is your first responsibility,' Xandine said. 'Nonetheless, since I have watched over you carefully these last days and weeks with my mystic arts, I know of what you speak. It will be of no hindrance to you. Indeed, the woman you seek may prove a boon. The city towards which you were travelling lies on the road to Kaandor and since the snows still close the passes, you can afford a small delay. But only a small one.' He stood abruptly, the robed and hooded personification of ancient sorcery. 'But before you go on your way, I must equip you with the weapons you will need.'

Fire*Wolf scowled. 'With this accursed sword, I have little need of weapons.'

For the first time, his father, the Lord Xandine, smiled. 'The weapons I have in mind are of a different nature. In order to defeat the Spawn, you must learn elements of sorcery.'

'No!' screamed Fire*Wolf in sudden alarm.

But the glittering eyes bored remorslessly into his soul. 'It is necessary,' Xandine said.

*So, despite his horror of the Arts, our Barbarian seems destined to become a sorcerer as well as a fighting man. Strange are the twists and turns of Destiny. Follow him now as Lord Xandine strides from the great hall with Fire*Wolf en train. Go, with bated breath, to* **119**.

104

The blade plunged.

Fire*Wolf experienced more surprise than pain before the final darkness claimed him.

Go to **13**.

105

The Doomsword howled as it arched viciously towards the woman's throat. She made no move to step aside, no move to resist. Her eyes, locked on Fire*Wolf's own, held no plea for mercy. The blade bit home . . .

There was no gush of blood, no severing of the slim neck. Instead, Fire*Wolf experienced a fierce jolt of pain in his arm.

Yveen smiled. 'Perchance you will not find me as easy to kill as you imagine.' With a gentle gesture, she hurled a bolt of fiery energy in his direction.

*Has Fire*Wolf bitten off more than he can chew? It would certainly seem so: but the die is cast now and only further die casting can get him out of trouble. Turn to Page 249 for Yveen's impressive stats. If*

*Fire**Wolf survives, he must go to* **97** *to listen to what she has to say. If not . . . well, there's always* **13**.

106

Working as much by touch as sight, Fire*Wolf searched diligently for any hidden mechanism that might open up a passage for him.

*A matter of luck as much as anything else. Thus you must roll two dice and multiply the result by eight. Compare the final total with Fire**Wolf's* LUCK *figure. If your score is higher, then our hero does not get lucky. Go to* **98** *and reconsider his options. If your score is lower, then go to* **108**.

107

After what seemed an eternity of searching, Fire*Wolf finally faced up to the truth: there was no secret door. Gloomily he climbed back through the hole in the ceiling and made his way back to the battlements.

Where we must follow him. Go to **55** *and reconsider his options.*

108

There was a sharp click as Fire*Wolf's questing fingers encountered the trigger of the ancient mechanism. He felt not simply a door, but the entire slab begin to move, sliding sideways with a scream of stone on stone.

When the way was clear, he moved onwards – and was halted almost at once by a second barrier identical to the first.

Nonplussed, Fire*Wolf began a second search. And as he did so, the explanation of the double barrier came to him. Since the secret entrance was below the level of the moat, some form of lock would have to be incorporated in the tunnel to prevent the castle flooding. He was obviously within that lock now.

His experience of finding the first mechanism helped him here.

In moments he had the trigger to the second. He pressed it firmly and experienced no surprise when the slab behind him ground across to seal the tunnel. For a nerve-racking instant, he wondered if the slab before him would open, or whether time had jammed the mechanism, leaving him trapped. But then he heard the grinding, felt the vibration. . .

Fire*Wolf was immediately pounded into shocked insensibility by the weight of water which struck him.

> *What a ghastly error! The tunnel was not a secret entrance into the castle, but rather the main water feed to the moat, disused these many years but still operative from the deep, powerful underground spring which feeds it. Trapped and battered by the force of water, our hero has no hope at all. Go to* **13**.

109

Fire*Wolf launched himself through the opening, already narrowing as the chamber revolved.

With all the speed he could muster, he ran towards the exit.

But how much SPEED *can he muster? And will it be enough? Roll two dice and multiply the result by eight. Compare your total with Fire*Wolf's* SPEED *figure. If the* SPEED *figure is higher, go to* **116**. *If lower, then go to* **117**.

110

Vainly Fire*Wolf struggled with the bond that held him to the cable. He could feel vibrations along its length, smell the rank odour of something horrible approaching from the dark depths of the pit. Two fiery, faceted eyes drew closer like twin brands carried at the head of a procession of the dead. Then the creature was upon him. He had a fleeting impression of waving, monstrous, hirsute legs, a face as ghastly as the tomb, fangs oozing venom.

Then it struck.

Go to **13**.

111

At once the door swung open.

Fire*Wolf started back towards the prisoner. 'Now,' he said, 'we are free to go.'

'You are free, Barbarian,' the fettered prisoner said. 'I am dead. Captivity and freedom have no meaning to me. Save yourself and find Lord Xandine – that is all I ask. Leave me here to rot.'

But Fire*Wolf was not listening. With all the ferocity in his Barbarian soul he flung himself upon the rusted fetters. Despite his attack, the chains held, but their fixings to the wall were weakened by damp and age and in a moment he had torn them loose. Without their support, the prisoner pitched forward in a huddled heap on the stone floor.

'Can you walk?' asked Fire*Wolf.

There was no answer. Fire*Wolf bent to examine the man. There was no pulse, no heartbeat. He was dead.

Fire*Wolf backed away in superstitious awe. Had he really been dead all the time? Certainly he was beyond help now. Without further delay he turned and headed for the open door.

As he did so, a whining sound like some gigantic insect reached him from the corridor beyond.

He hesitated, then drew the Doomsword and moved forward. It was his only option.

The corridor ran straight and true for fifty yards, then opened into a doorless, circular chamber. It was from this chamber that the whining noise emerged. As Fire*Wolf drew closer, he saw that the cause was mechanical: the floor of the chamber was spinning like a turntable – and not just the floor. The entire chamber was turning!

In the moment it took for Fire*Wolf to comprehend what he was watching, realization of his predicament abruptly dawned. There was an open exit at the far side of the chamber, an open entrance just a yard or two before him. But as the chamber turned, both would be sealed in seconds, leaving him trapped again. Did he have time to cross the chamber before the exit sealed? Should he even try – and risk being trapped within the chamber itself – or should he remain where he was and attempt to discover the secret of the mechanism?

Fire*Wolf stood locked in indecision.

But he cannot remain so locked forever. If he decides to stay put and search for the mechanism, go to **118**. *If he decides to risk a dash across the chamber, race with him to* **109**.

112

Fire*Wolf turned and began to walk silently from the great hall, his back crawling at the thought of what magic Xandine could hurl towards him. Father or no, he did not trust this sorcerer.

But Xandine only called, 'Hold!'

Fire*Wolf hesitated, then stopped. As he turned, he said, 'I cannot do as you say. I am bound on another course.'

'That,' said Xandine, 'I know already. But let me say this: the Time Lock, as I told you, has already begun to crumble. Only a sorcerer can survive the disaster that will follow. I am dying and can protect you, this castle and this valley only a little longer. If you leave now, you are doomed.'

*Interesting information . . . if it is true. Fire*Wolf has an opportunity to change his mind. If he does, go to* **119**. *If he insists on going his own way, go to* **120**.

113

The rotting mortar shattered. Fire*Wolf kicked out violently to give himself momentum and, in a shower of dust and brickwork, broke through into a small chamber, with stone walls and a wooden floor.

Fire*Wolf climbed slowly to his feet. There was little to see. The room appeared empty and deserted, dust covered and disused. But there was, at least, a door opening out of it.

Fire*Wolf started towards it . . . and the wooden flooring collapsed beneath his feet!

> *This is no small thing for our hero. It may, in fact, quite easily kill him. Throw two dice. Multiply the result by eight and compare it with his* LUCK *figure. If the* LUCK figure is higher, go to **101**. *If not, it's the dreaded* **13**.

114

'In that case,' said the crone, 'handsome lad that you are, I must tussle with you!'

Instinctively, Fire*Wolf's hand dropped to the handle of his sword. But the old woman did not move. Instead, she began to croon – a soft sound, like a mother's lullaby.

Fire*Wolf stared at her in amazement, wondering if she had gone mad. But the sound swept over him and the old woman's eyes grew large and he felt his limbs becoming heavy.

'Don't worry, my brave warrior,' the crone murmured quietly. 'You're in no danger from me. No danger at all . . .'

And the room swam about him . . .

Go to **72**.

115

On his fifth attempt, he felt the wall before him crumble. Minutes later he had opened a hole wide enough to crawl through. But before he had moved many yards beyond this barrier, he found another.

And was immediately pounded into shocked insensibility by the weight of water which struck him.

What a ghastly error! The tunnel was not a secret entrance into the castle, but rather the main water feed to the moat, disused these many years but still operative from the deep, powerful underground spring which feeds it. Trapped and battered by the force of water, our hero has no hope at all. Go to **13**.

116

Fire∗Wolf leaped through as the revolving chamber closed the exit behind him.

And fell!

For an eternity he tumbled through space and darkness before the darkness leeched into his mind and he lost consciousness completely.

Go to **44**.

117

He crashed headlong into solid wall as the exit closed before him. The revolving floor carried him a little distance before its movement and the whining stopped.

118

Fire*Wolf lay, half stunned, then picked himself up slowly and explored his surroundings.

There was no way out.

No way at all. Our hero's physical attributes have let him down with a vengeance. He will survive for quite a while, of course, but lacking limitless supplies of food and water, the result must be inevitable. Go to **13**.

118

The entrance sealed itself as the whining stopped and the chamber ceased to revolve.

At once, Fire*Wolf set about to find the mechanism.

But as the minutes stretched to hours, he was forced to face up to his mistake. Wherever the mechanism lay, it did not lie within his reach. Before him was a sealed exit. Behind him only the cell he had so recently vacated.

His future stretched before him: a long, slow road to starvation and death.

Go to **13**.

INTO THE CRYPTS

119

'There is little time,' Xandine said. 'Already I am aware of the Time Lock crumbling and I can do less and less to sustain it. We must at once begin your education as a sorcerer. Nothing less can stand against the Demonspawn and even with sorcery to aid you, there is no guarantee you will overcome them. But we must try . . .'

'Lord Xandine,' Fire*Wolf said tentatively, still unwilling to use the appellation 'father', 'I have no taste for sorcery, nor any knowledge of the Arts.'

'That I know full well. And there is too little time to train you as I myself was trained. But there is a way – not without risk, but swift.'

'What is this way?'

'All sorcery,' said Xandine gravely, 'is no more than the application of power. Power itself is universal, but so diffuse that it is useless for any practical purpose. When a man becomes a sorcerer, he learns to draw the universal power into himself and, so to speak, condense it within his body. Once this is achieved, the power may then be drawn upon as necessary. The more power a man has managed to accumulate, the greater sorcerer he becomes.'

119

'But how,' asked Fire*Wolf, 'is this power accumulated?'

'In normal circumstances very slowly,' Xandine told him. 'The human body is unused to power and can disintegrate completely if too much is fed in too quickly. But these are not normal circumstances. We have to find a means of completing your training in hours or days rather than years. And that leaves only the Ordeal.'

'The Ordeal?' echoed Fire*Wolf.

'It is a method used in certain cultures, most of them quite primitive. When a man is seen destined for sorcery, he is subjected to a ritual Ordeal which makes him at once receptive to a massive inflow of power and at the same time toughens his mind and body sufficiently to receive it. But it is the essence of the Ordeal that it is a test of mind and body – and a dangerous test. Most fail it and die.'

'And if I fail?' asked Fire*Wolf.

'Then we are all doomed,' Xandine said.

They walked together from the audience hall, through an ante-chamber and down a broad flight of stone steps to a marbled entrance hall. Twin doors stood before them, but Xandine turned in another direction.

'Within this castle,' he said, 'are many areas fraught with danger to the unwary. But none so dangerous as its Crypts. These I have personally designed, through ingenuity and Art, to provide the ultimate test of any man.' He paused before a stout oakwood door, bound in iron, and produced from the folds of his robe a heavy metal key. 'Beyond this entrance is a flight of steps downwards. They lead to the Crypts. This is where you must enter, Fire*Wolf: and you must enter both naked and unarmed.'

'I cannot leave the Doomsword,' Fire*Wolf said. 'It is bound to me by some magic I do not understand.'

'Your sword will not accompany you into the Crypts, even if you wish it,' Xandine told him confidently. 'The forces which play below would not permit it entry. However, if you survive, the sword will await you when you leave – although you will have less use of it then than hithertofore.'

'When I enter, what must I do?'

'Simply survive,' Xandine told him. 'Seek the exit, which will lead you not only beyond this castle, but beyond the valley. You may then discharge your obligation to the hermit with your quest for his lost daughter. After that you must seek out and face the Spawn. If you survive the Crypts, you will be better equipped for both tasks. If not . . .' He left the sentence incomplete, nor did he need to finish it.

Fire*Wolf took a deep breath. 'Open the door,' he said.

> *Thus, almost casually, our hero embarks on a new adventure which must change his life or put an end to it entirely. Follow him into the Crypts by turning to* **150**.

120

But Fire*Wolf only shrugged and walked from the great chamber, still half expecting some form of magical attack that never came.

He was, he discovered, in a part of the castle he had not seen before, although common sense told him he must have passed this way to reach the chamber. It was an open ante-chamber, furnished with the trappings of great wealth, a place where once visitors might have waited to pay court to the Lord. But now, the trappings were faded, showing signs of decay. There was a skeleton reclining on a pile of oriental cushions near the door. As he passed it, some errant imagination made him think it moved, but when he looked directly, all he saw was the bleached bones.

It was, he knew, important to leave the castle as quickly as possible – to leave the valley itself. For even if Xandine were lying about the Time Lock, it was obvious that Fire*Wolf would be best served by putting as much distance as possible between this accursed place and himself.

He left the ante-chamber and paused at the head of a grand staircase, sweeping downwards to what could only be a marbled entrance hall. Ahead, he could see the great doors which might lead to the outside.

He started down the staircase and felt the steps begin to crumble beneath his feet.

Fire*Wolf ran.

There were people moving from corridors into the entrance hall – young women mainly, with a scattering of men. He blinked, for his first impression had been mistaken: they were not young, but rather middle-aged – no, old.

The stairs were crumbling, sending him pitching forward, clutching at a balustrade which itself was crumbling.

The people in the entrance hall were falling, dying. . . He saw one change in an instant from a beautiful young maiden to a pile of bones similar to that which had lain on the oriental cushions.

He heard, but did not feel, a rushing wind. Somewhere, distantly, someone or something was screaming. The words 'Time Lock' came strongly to his mind. At his side, the Doomsword began to howl, thirsting for life force in some dreadful arcane extremity. He could not keep his feel. He was falling. Around him the very fabric of the castle seemed to shimmer, crumble. . . .

And so the Time Lock passed away and with it, unfortunately, our mistrusting hero. Go to **13**.

121

As he turned his eyes away from the crystal, Fire*Wolf caught sight of a faint inscription cut into the rough pedestal on which the statue stood. It was difficult to read, but close inspection finally allowed him to make out the wording.

It was, to his surprise, a poem.

All ye who enter in this room
Have entered in the Crypts of Doom.
You search for Power, with vision bold
But I, a beggar, search for gold.
Your entrance will your exit be
Provided you can place the fee
Upon the crystal gem I hold.

Fire*Wolf scratched the stubble of his beard. The words were plain enough, but their meaning was cryptic. This was the entrance chamber and it had no fewer than five exits, all of them apparently unguarded. But even if they had been locked and barred, there was no way in which he could provide a fee in gold to place on the beggar's hand. Had he not been stripped of his possessions in preparation for the Ordeal?

Fire*Wolf stood up. He was not a patient man and he had more stomach for action than riddles. There were five open exits. He was not so naive as to imagine any one of them would lead him directly to the outside. But one must be the right route eventually.

Which to choose . . .?

*Which indeed! For convenience, we will number the exits 1 to 5, since any one looks much like any other. You must now choose for Fire*Wolf and may the gods guide your intuition. If Exit 1 go to* **129**. *If 2 then* **137**. *If 3 then* **145**. *If 4 then* **156**. *If 5 then* **170**.

122

Fire*Wolf breathed the clear, sweet taste of fresh air in his lungs. He was not entirely sure how he had reached this place, but he felt strong, brim-full of energy. He felt *good*!

As well he might. Please turn to Special Section A on page 242 for full details of what our hero has achieved.

123

The lid of the sixth chest flew open. Fire*Wolf approached it cautiously. Inside lay a single glittering golden coin.

123

*And with this coin in his possession, Fire*Wolf will now discover the exit door of the chamber opens easily. Go to* **180**.

A STRANGER IN BELGARDIUM

124

There were many changes in the Barbarian since he had stumbled from the Wilderness that had shaped so many of his ways. Indeed, to superficial appearances, he scarcely warranted to be called 'Barbarian' at all.

Several of the changes were obvious. He no longer strode half-naked through the countryside of Harn. Now he wore robes which, but for his muscular build and the wild look about his eyes, might immediately have marked him as a merchant. The Doomsword remained by his side, locked to him by the bonds of sorcery and Destiny, but now it was well hidden by the sweep and folds of his travelling cloak. He no longer walked, but rode, his mount a jet-black stallion which had been the last gift of his dying father Xandine before the Time Lock crumbled and the accursed castle and enchanted valley finally fell to ruin. And he had gold in his purse for the first time in his life – enough gold to ensure his welcome at any inn or hostelry throughout the land.

But certain of the changes were more subtle. He seemed taller somehow, a change occasioned by the way he held himself. He had always been a handsome man, a man who cut an impressive figure in any company. But now there was added an aura of subtle authority. He no longer seemed so restless, so nervously watchful like some great beast which had momentarily found itself outside its natural habitat. He looked, in short, like a man who knew who he was and where he was going. Perhaps it was the knowledge of his bloodline, or the sorcerous powers he had earned at the risk of his life. Perhaps it was something given, a subtle donation by Xandine along with horse and gold. Perhaps it was simply the acceptance of his convoluted Destiny, which must lead him first to Belgardium, then, when he succeeded in his quest for Baldar's daughter, to the dark, looming mountains which bordered Harn and gave the only access to the perils of Kaandor. Whatever had caused it, it was there.

He rode through countryside that changed slowly as the days went by. At first signs of human habitation had been rare. Now they became increasingly frequent – cottages, farmsteads, houses. Eventually he reached an inn and realized he need no longer spend another night beneath the stars. More to the point, he could also find specific directions to Belgardium, for until now, while he knew he was travelling in the rough direction of the coastal city, he did not know for certain which were the best roads to follow.

He swung his stallion into the cobbled courtyard, dismounted and called loudly for the landlord. His call was answered by a slim, small weasel of a man with shifty looks who emerged from the interior with an obsequious smile to bid the visitor welcome.

But Fire*Wolf had no eyes for the landlord, for behind him, framed in the doorway, was a burly, black-bearded figure Fire*Wolf recognized instantly. It was Tojar the Slaver. Who knew how many of his companions were inside?

What does Fire∗Wolf do now? A swift attack would certainly dispatch Tojar and allow immediate escape. Or our hero might bank on the fact that in his new raiment he would be unrecognizable to this ruffian. The choice, as always, is yours. If Fire∗Wolf attacks, go to **127**. *If not, then go to* **163**.

125

Fire∗Wolf reached out for the crystal. As his fingers touched the surface of the glowing gem, there was an abrupt and silent explosion of blue light. With appalling violence, Fire∗Wolf was flung backwards against the bare stone wall.

For a moment he lay stunned, then slowly picked himself up again. The statue stood as before, the crystal still glowing in its palm. Fire∗Wolf examined himself carefully and found no bones were broken, although he felt weak. With a ringing in his ears, he moved back towards the statue.

Weak indeed. Fire∗Wolf has lost one quarter of his current LIFE POINTS. *And his decision still remains. Should he make another attempt to take the crystal, hoping its guardian violence has now been discharged? Or should he leave it alone? If you wish him to make another attempt, then go to* **162**. *If not, go to* **121**.

126

The box explodes. Go to **13**.

127

Faster than the speed of thought, the Doomsword was in Fire*Wolf's hand. In a bound he was past the landlord and launching himself at Tojar. The big man was taken completely by surprise, so that he fell back in alarm, scrabbling for his own weapon.

*But surprised or not, Tojar remains a formidable opponent. Check his stats on page 249, allow Fire*Wolf the first strike, then calculate the result of this combat. If Fire*Wolf loses, go to* **13**. *If he wins, turn to* **134**.

128

Swiftly they wound the bed linen into a soundly knotted rope, tied one end to the heavy bedleg and dropped the other through the window.

Fire*Wolf paused on the sill. 'I have to thank you. What is your name?'

'Landa,' the girl said.

'Then I thank you, Landa, and ask one more thing from you. The Northerners who seek to kill me – do they have captives in their charge?'

Landa nodded.

'Where are they imprisoned?'

'In the stables,' said the girl.

Without another word, Fire*Wolf climbed from the window.

He reached the yard without mishap. The stable blocks had outside bolts, but no proper locks. Fortune was with him, for on the first door he tried, he found his stallion. Working with feverish intensity, he saddled the animal and led it quietly outside. Next he carefully unbarred each door of the block, taking care not to disturb the animals inside. If he was to flee these men, the least he could do was to ensure pursuit was difficult and he had a plan in mind for that.

But first, there was something else to do. Methodically, he began to search for the stable which held the slavers' captives. He still had not found it when a gruff voice called, 'What are you doing?'

Fire*Wolf swung round to find himself facing Tojar, flanked on one side by another of the black-bearded Northerners and on the other by the landlord, no longer obsequious but with a slim blade glittering in his hand.

*Fight or flee? Again the decision presents itself. Fire*Wolf wishes to free the slaves, but now to do so he will have to fight these three men, with every chance that the noise will attract the rest of their companions and who knows who else. He can, however, reach his stallion easily and be well away before these ruffians truly realise what is happening. If he fights, check the stats of his opponents on Page 249 and calculate the outcome. Death leaves him back at* **13**. *If he wins, go to* **149**. *Should he decide to flee, go to* **139**.

129

He stepped into a narrow corridor which ran north east for little more than thirty feet before turning due east.

At first he hesitated, not liking the confined space or the low level of the light, but then it occurred to him that there was little he could do if attacked by some creature here. The Doomsword, as Xandine had predicted, was no longer with him. He had neither arms nor armour, only his wits and skill. It might not prove enough, but it was all he had.

Fire*Wolf took a deep breath and strode onwards.

The eastern corridor took him to the entrance of a chamber twenty foot square, empty of furnishings, empty of everything else in fact except for a solitary gold coin glinting in the middle of the floor. At the far side of the chamber was an open exit.

Without hesitation, Fire*Wolf stepped inside.

At once, the ceiling high above crashed down upon him, seeming in that heart-stopping instant to be set to squash him like an insect on the floor. Instinctively, Fire*Wolf threw himself flat – and to his profound relief, the downward plunge of the ceiling halted no more than four feet above his head.

But the relief was short-lived, for now Fire*Wolf saw that as the ceiling had come down, so thick metal bars has risen from the floor to seal both his entrance and exit.

What now?

He crawled to the exit (with enough presence of mind to take the gold coin from the floor) and tested the bars. They were firmly imbedded, but he thought he might have just enough strength to bend them. He determined to try. It was, after all, his only hope.

But has he enough STRENGTH? *Only you can tell. Roll two dice and multiply the result by eight. Compare this total with our hero's* STRENGTH *figure. If his* STRENGTH *figure is higher, then he can bend the bars and escape with his coin to* **180**. *If not, he rots. Go to* **13**.

130

Fire*Wolf stood upright. His eyes had now grown accustomed to the darkness so that he could make out the faint outlines of simple furnishings – a bed, a locker, a heavily curtained window, a door. . .

He tried the door and found, without surprise, that it was locked. He was half way towards the curtained window when a faint sound halted him. It was the gentle grating of a key in a lock. He turned in time to see a widening chink of light as the door slowly opened.

The Doomsword was still in his hand.

And he has the opportunity to use it in a surprise attack on his captors. Should he do so? If your decision is yes, then go to **138**. *If he waits to find out who is coming, go to* **167**.

131

Fire*Wolf cleaned his sword amid the carnage. Behind him he heard a soft footfall on the stair, but when he turned it was the landlord's daughter, Landa, eyes wide in horror at the sight before her.

Frowning, Fire*Wolf muttered, 'I am sorry about your father. He attacked me and I had no alternative.'

To his surprise, she shrugged. 'He was my step-father only and an evil man. You have done me a service in taking his life.'

'But what will become of you?'

'I have the inn. I am young, but I have helped him run it for four years and I can certainly run it alone now. What of you, Merchant, if you are a merchant . . .?'

Fire*Wolf ignored the unspoken question. 'I have business to attend to. First, the slaves these men took must be freed. You know where they are held?'

'In the stables at the back,' Landa told him. 'I shall release them at once.'

'And I,' said Fire*Wolf, 'shall clean up this chaos.'

*An interesting aside to his destined adventure and one that, fortuitously, ended cleanly. But now Fire*Wolf has more important things to do. Go to* **135**.

132

The lid of the fourth chest flew open and the first chest vanished in the flicker of an eye.

Fire*Wolf bent to examine the open chest and found it empty. What now?

What now is simple: he can roll the die again. Any score of 1 or of 4 should be ignored. On 2 go to **175**. *On 3 go to* **141**. *On 5 go to* **148**. *On 6 go to* **123**.

133

'No!' Fire*Wolf exclaimed. 'To run from such men is to run forever.' He pushed past the startled girl, flung the door wide and hurled himself down the wooden stairs, the Doomsword howling exultantly in his hand.

The slaver band, black-bearded and black-robed as he remembered them, were in the tavern below, drinking ale by the light of oil lamps. His sudden, wild appearance took them completely by surprise, so that three were dead beneath the onslaught of the Doomsword before any had time to react. Of the remainder in the room, two were unarmed and one drunk so that they fled screaming in alarm.

But two remained, who fell upon Fire*Wolf like Furies. And even as they attacked, the landlord appeared from a back room, sword in hand.

> *So Fire*Wolf's attack has not proved so rash as it might. But three enemies remain to be dispatched. Check their stats on page 249 and calculate the outcome. Fire*Wolf will have to dispatch all three. If he fails and is killed, go to* **13**. *If he succeeds, go to* **131**.

134

Fire*Wolf felt the flow of energy erupt from his Doomsword as the man died from the final thrust. And in that very instant, the universe seemed to explode in a searing blast of pain. Then darkness claimed him.

He awoke groggily in a darkened room, arms and legs securely bound. His head thumped abominably. After a moment he collected his thoughts despite the pain and murmured quietly, 'Doombringer. . .?'

'I am here, Barbarian,' the suave voice echoed in his mind.

'What happened?'

'The landlord struck you from behind, then called the slaver's companions. They gave him your gold as a reward.'

'So I am captive in the inn?'

'Yes.'

'Where are you?' Fire*Wolf asked. 'I cannot see you.'

'Behind you, Barbarian. They took me away, of course, but through the links of Destiny and sorcery, I have returned.'

'Can you cut me free?'

'I am powerless without your touch, Barbarian,' the smooth voice said.

At once, Fire*Wolf began to wriggle in the direction his instincts told him the Doomsword lay. Eventually his bound hands reached it. 'Now!' he hissed.

The sword hummed quietly, then twisted in his grip and sliced the bonds around his legs as if they had been thread. A wave of nausea swept through Fire*Wolf's body. Realization struck him instantly. It was in the nature of the sword to drink life energies when it was used. In the absence of an enemy, this use was charged to Fire*Wolf's own reserves.

135

But there was no other course. Gagging, Fire*Wolf murmured, 'Now my hands.'

'Of course,' the smooth voice whispered in his mind.

*This is possibly a more dangerous business than even Fire*Wolf imagines. Each usage of the Doom-sword will absorb* LIFE POINTS *equivalent to a double dice roll multiplied by four. And Fire*Wolf is on his second usage. Make the necessary rolls and calculations. If Fire*Wolf's total* LIFE POINTS *are absorbed, go to* **13**. *If not, he may stagger on to* **130**.

135

Dawn broke to find Fire*Wolf already on the road, gripped by a curious, instinctive sense of urgency. His stallion too seemed unusually nervous, for the great horse plunged and snorted as if threatening to unseat him at every turn.

The road was deserted at this hour – on reflection, he realized he had seen amazingly few travellers at any time since he left the inn and his old friends the slavers. This was curious, since he knew now that he was approaching close to the coastal city of Belgardium, a huge population centre and the focus of a great many trade routes. There should surely have been many more travellers by now: merchant caravans, pilgrims, mercenaries, mendicant friars, fortune hunters . . . the whole ragbag of wanderers for whom the great port would act as a lodestone. Yet there were none. He might have been the only soul left in all of Harn if he were to judge solely by the company he discovered on the road.

An errant thought prompted him to wonder if he might have lost his way. But he had maps now, provided by the Wizard Xandine who claimed to be his father; and those maps had proven themselves quite accurate so far. Landmark after landmark had appeared exactly as predicted. Even now, the road was climbing as the map indicated it should. Soon he would top the rise and look down over the whole of the ancient crater in which Belgardium now nestled as it hugged the natural inlet on the coastline which had determined its destiny as a major trading centre.

The stallion reared abruptly, then stopped stock still, quivering. Fire*Wolf too froze into immobility, listening. The beast was not by nature temperamental and he realized something was disturbing it greatly. With ears much keener than his own, it had, perhaps, picked up a sound.

And in a moment, Fire*Wolf heard it too. The distant clink of harness, a rumbling like the first hint of an earthquake; and finally, chillingly, the faint sound of sorrow, like the ghastly chorus of souls in torment.

It was this latter noise which had disturbed the stallion. As it increased in volume, the great black horse grew increasingly nervous until Fire*Wolf was forced to dismount and stand beside its head, whispering in its ear to calm it down.

He was stood thus, right hand hovering habitually within reach of the Doomsword, when in the cold grey light of morning, the first intimation of a great disaster topped the rise ahead.

*But what? No choice to make here. Simply hurry to find out what Fire*Wolf saw by turning now to* **143**.

136

Thus an exhausted Fire*Wolf staggered from the inn to find his stallion. In the stables he discovered the slavers' captives and released them with a sense, a curious sense, of subtle defeat.

But he was resilient and knew his destiny. The road to Belgardium still lay before him.

Go to **135**.

137

The corridor ran north west before turning directly west. Fire*Wolf followed it with considerable trepidation until it ended in a wooden door. Half expecting it to be locked, he tried the handle, and found it opened easily.

He was in a large rectangular chamber with a single exit. Set at intervals along the floor were six metal bound wooden chests. Near them lay a huge crystal die, each face almost a foot square, the numbering picked out in ruby inlay: a magical artifact if ever Fire*Wolf saw one.

He tried the chests and found he could not open them. He tried the exit door and found it locked. He returned to the door through which he had entered and found it too barred against him.

After a moment, Fire*Wolf picked up the crystal die . . .

No, it doesn't explode or otherwise incapacitate him. It is, in fact, the key to his Ordeal of Luck. Roll one (non-crystal) die on his behalf to determine if he survives the present Ordeal. Score 1 and go to **166**. *Score 2 and go to* **175**. *Score 3 and go to* **141**. *Score 4 and go to* **132**. *Score 5 and go to* **148**. *Score 6 and go to* **123**.

138

The Doomsword arched and howled.

The intruder did not stand a chance as the demon blade drank deeply of his soul. The body fell at Fire*Wolf's feet, illuminated by the pool of light that streamed in from outside the room.

Except that this was no slaver, no landlord, not a man at all, but a slim young girl of no more than sixteen years.

Sickened, Fire*Wolf turned away from the bloody corpse. But the deed was done now and there was no recalling the dead to life.

Or was there? An outwardly directed RESURRECTION *spell might do the trick, if Fire*Wolf has the* POWER *to try it. Should he decide to do so and the spell prove positive, go to* **167**. *Should he decide not, or the spell fail, go to* **147**.

139

Fire*Wolf acted without a moment's hesitation. He ran towards the group howling with such ferocity that they fell back in momentary alarm. But he did not strike at them , did not attempt to strike. Instead he seized his opportunity to break past them and vault on to the back of his waiting stallion.

140

The gateway and escape lay open before him. But he ignored the obvious to ride towards the stables. Clinging to his horse's mane and using all the skill he possessed, he flung open door after door at a gallop, screaming as he did so.

In a moment the courtyard was a melee of milling mounts and fleeing slaves. Smiling grimly to himself, Fire*Wolf wheeled his stallion and raced for the gateway. There would be no fast pursuit that night. He was on his way again.

Indeed he was. Go to **135**.

140

*(Add one point to Fire*Wolf's* SKILL*)*

Baldar picked himself up, grinning sheepishly. 'It seems I underestimated you, Fungus Feeder,' he remarked. 'Not a warrior with much finesse, but a fighter of some determination.' He shrugged. 'Still, it's one thing to best an old man – quite another to survive the rigours of Belgardium.'

'Belgardium?' Fire*Wolf echoed, panting a little, for in truth the old hermit had proven a far tougher opponent than he had imagined.

'A town of generous proportions or a city of mean ones, depending on your viewpoint,' Baldar said. 'It has few claims to fame and only one of any great importance – I lived there for many years before I discovered my own company was preferable to that of thieves and scoundrels. I had a mind to send you there.'

Fire*Wolf squatted with his back against a nearby boulder, eyeing the old man warily. 'Why should I wish to go to Belgardium?'

'Well, I might say because you owe me your life and even a Wilderness Barbarian must have some sense of obligation. Or I might say only that you're young and restless, an adventurous spirit with nowhere to go, so that Belgardium is as good a destination as any.'

'You might say all that with truth, Hermit,' agreed Fire*Wolf sagely. 'But then I should have to ask you why you wish me to go to Belgardium.'

'Now that requires a fuller answer. Let us return to the cave and I shall give it to you.'

Go to **144**.

141

The lid of the third chest flew open. Simultaneously, and with frightening precision, the remaining chests disappeared, flickering out of existence like a candle-flame in a sudden gust of wind.

Fire*Wolf looked into the remaining chest.

It was empty.

*No reward for Fire*Wolf here. He will, however, now find he can open the exit door. The corridor beyond will carry him to the chamber of the statue, from whence he may choose a new exit he has not previously taken, or choose to return to the chamber of the crystal die and chests. The*

Section numbers are **129** *. . .* **137** *(die and chests exit) . . .* **145** *. . .* **156** *. . .* **170***.*

142

Go to **133***.*

143

They came in their scores, their hundreds, their thousands . . .ragged,bleeding,stumbling men, women, children, their pitiful possessions piled on wooden carts, some pushed feebly by the people themselves, some drawn by mules or horses.

There were young and old here, rich and poor, columns of wounded soldiery held partially together by some faint memory of discipline, merchants once sleek with wealth, now stripped of their old finery, a scattering of aristocrats with no more than their noble bearing to distinguish them now from the common herd. There were men and women half-naked, shivering in the chill morning air, warriors with broken weapons and suppurating wounds, priests stumbling as they told their beads and mumbled prayers to their uncaring gods. They held to the road with the grim determination of marching ants, but there was no cohesion here, no purpose. They stumbled, staggered and those who fell were not helped to their feet again, but lay and rose of their own accord, or did not rise at all. There was fear on every face, from the youngest child to the most venerable ancient; and of them all, the priests seemed most fearful. Exhaustion was plainly written on every face, yet they hurried, dear gods, how they hurried, pushing themselves beyond the outmost limits of human endurance as if nothing else mattered but movement onwards.

And out of this fearful, ghastly caravan there arose a muted wail of anguish as its members voiced their last remaining protest to the heavens.

'Hold!' Fire*Wolf called and was ignored. The stumbling figures streamed past him as if he were no more than a milestone on the road. None turned to look towards him. None acknowledged his presence in any way.

'What has happened?' Fire*Wolf shouted in mounting alarm. Who were these people? Whence did they come? What disaster had befallen them? He stepped forward directly into the path of an old, frail priest, caught his arm, dragged him to a halt.

And only when he looked into those pain-filled eyes did Fire*Wolf realize that the man was blind. Some instinct made him swing his head and instantly the suspicion was confirmed. All were blind. Every one. Men, women, children – all sightless, following some inner vision or fleeing from some dark nightmare with orbs like cooked albumen set into the sockets of their skulls.

'What happened?' Fire*Wolf asked the priest, more gently this time.

The old man muttered like one far gone in delirium. For a moment Fire*Wolf thought he would receive no lucid answer. Then some semblance of ancient faith gave the priest strength enough to answer and he enunciated a single word which encompassed a universe of meaning:

143

'Spawn!'

'The Demonspawn?' asked Fire*Wolf.

'In the night they attacked Belgardium. The city is in ruins.'

Stunned, Fire*Wolf released his arm. The priest stumbled back into the wailing crowd and staggered onwards in the communal flight from the disaster. The Spawn had attacked Belgardium? But it was impossible! Xandine had warned him there was little time, but promised there was some. The Harkaan could not move until the mountain passes were clear of the winter snows and two full weeks or more remained before the seasonal thaw. Yet the Demonspawn had come and laid waste to a city. How?

In an instant of realization, Fire*Wolf felt his Destiny crash in upon him like a rockfall. Where was his obligation to the hermit Baldar now? Was Yalena one of these blind refugees? Or was she dead, lying broken in the ruins of Belgardium, beyond help or rescue? And could he even afford to consider Yalena now? She was no more than a name to him, a vision in the mind of her hermit father who could not know for certain if she were even in Belgardium when the Spawn attacked. What did he, Fire*Wolf, owe Baldar anyway? The man had saved his life, but that seemed an eternity ago in another place and did not the early appearance of the Spawn far outweigh all other considerations? Should he not now forget this hermit's daughter and concentrate his whole attention on his more important task?

*Convoluted are the threads of Fire*Wolf's Destiny. But what to do? Should he continue on to*

Belgardium to seek a corpse? Or should he attempt to discover more about the Spawn attack by questioning these blind refugees? If he goes to Belgardium, turn to **146**. *If he questions the refugees, go to* **151**.

144

In the cave, Baldar stretched out on the straw, as if his exertions had taken more of his energy than had been immediately apparent. Nonetheless, his voice was strong enough as he said, 'Do not think because you find me scratching on the edges of the Wilderness like a nomad that I was always thus, Fire*Wolf. I prefer my own company, as you know. But it may be that I should never have discovered this were it not for a series of misfortunes which befell me many years ago.

'I was a young man once, headstrong and tough, even as you are. I left the village where I was born and ventured into the world of Harn to make my fortune. Fate took me to Belgardium where I did indeed prosper, but at the expense of others, so that I made certain enemies, some highly placed. Not that this worried me. I was, as I say, headstrong. I was also in love: a great distraction from practical matters. I married the woman after some difficulties with her family and we lived happily for two years before she died bearing our first and only child, a daughter we had decided to name Yalena.

'The birth of Yalena gave me little joy – I was too heartbroken at the loss of my wife. I placed the child in care and plunged into my business activities in order to dull the pain. At that time, perceiving me weak and distracted, my most powerful enemies struck against me. The details are unimportant. Enough to tell you that I was forced to flee, leaving Yalena behind and taking with me only a tiny fraction of my amassed fortune. Even this I quickly lost so that for a time I wandered Harn surviving on my wits and, later, on my developed skill as a fighter. I sent many a good man beyond the Veil of Death in those days, Fire*Wolf, for I was both bitter and vicious.

'But the time came when I grew tired of killing, and more tired still of those who hired me to kill. I met an old woman, who must be long dead now. Her name was Coranna, although few knew it: they called her the Witch, sometimes the Oracle. I was a disbeliever in those days, but I found she had the Power all right. She read my past as a monk might read a scroll and though we had little in common, befriended me. It was she who sent me here to the Wilderness edge, having seen by her Arts that certain of my old enemies still pursued me and would assuredly take my life.

'Coranna predicted I would end my days here by the edge of the Wilderness, but that I would live happier while I lived here than at any time previously. I believed neither prediction then, although I believe them both now. A life such as I lead changes a man, makes him strong and self-sufficient, grants him vision and philosophy. These gifts are more precious than gold, Fire*Wolf; and ultimately more satisfying even than adventure.

'So you find me. And at any other time you would find me uncaring of the world and its woes. But a day and a night before you stumbled half-dead over my horizon, I had a dream. I dreamed of my daughter, Yalena, now a woman and as beautiful as her mother ever was. I dreamed great danger threatened her, although the nature of the danger I could not divine. In my dream I knew that if her life was to be saved she must be hidden in a place so dangerous that no man would dare to follow her. The name of this place was revealed to me as Kraal.'

'Kraal?' echoed Fire*Wolf, captivated by the old man's tale.

'Its nature and location are unknown to me,' Baldar admitted, 'although I have travelled more widely than most in Harn. Nonetheless, I know it to exist for I know I dreamed true.'

'How is it that you know you dreamed true, Old Man?' Fire*Wolf asked cautiously.

'Because I saw another in my dream alongside fair Yalena. I saw a fierce young Fungus Eater from the cold caves of the Deep Wilderness. I saw you, Fire*Wolf: and did you not come to me, half-dead though you were, in a day and a night?' He leaned forward, face and voice betraying his anxiety for the first time. 'Will you travel to Belgardium, Fire*Wolf? Will you seek out Yalena and take her from that cursed place? Will you undertake to find the place called Kraal and hide her there? Will you, Fire*Wolf? Will you?'

*Will you, Fire*Wolf? Will you accept the tangled web of Fate offered by this ancient hermit? You are free to refuse, to seek your destiny elsewhere. What do you really owe this Baldar? A fortuitous drink of water? A taste of nauseating food? But make up your* *own mind, Fire*Wolf. If you decide to undertake the task he wishes to set you, go to* **10**. *If you determine to refuse, go to* **1**.

145

The corridor ran east, then turned abruptly south. Fire*Wolf followed it until he reached the entrance of an elongated chamber. In the middle of the floor was a single glittering gold piece. But between Fire*Wolf and the gold was the most sinister mechanism he had ever seen . . .

Swinging from the ceiling of the chamber were three huge pendulums, each equipped with a shining, razor sharp, double-edged metal blade. The pendulums were set some twenty feet apart and their rate of swing differed slightly one from the other so that at no time was there a clear passage through.

Fortunately, just inside the doorway he had entered and well clear of the pendulums was a lever with two settings, one clearly marked ON, the other OFF. Fire*Wolf stepped inside and pushed the lever to the OFF position. The blades continued to swing, but the door behind him slammed shut, trapping him. But at least he could now see, beyond the blades, an open exit.

But how to reach it? SPEED *would seem to be the only answer, yet the calculations of success or failure are by no means simple. Obviously we begin with Fire*Wolf's* SPEED *figure. Equally obviously, we must roll dice on behalf of the blades. We may rest assured that if a blade does strike him on his run he will be instant macedoine. (And go to* **13**.*) Now roll two dice on behalf of the blades and* *multiply the result by eight. Check Fire*Wolf's* SPEED *figure, then use the following table to make comparisons:*

*Fire*Wolf's* SPEED	*Blades strike on*
90 – 96	85 or better
80 – 89	75 or better
70 – 79	65 or better
60 – 69	55 or better
50 – 59	45 or better
40 – 49	35 or better
30 – 39	25 or better
20 – 29	15 or better
Below 20	Certain hit

*If Fire*Wolf survives, he may take the coin en passant and go to* **180**. *If not, as we have previously noted, it is* **13** *for him.*

146

It was with a guilty feeling of relief that Fire*Wolf left the tragic caravan behind. But the relief was short-lived. Streams of refugees continued to emerge from the direction of the stricken city, most of them blind like those he had first met, others sighted but covered in sores as if stricken by some horrendous plague. Still others were crippled or reduced by the horror of their experience to walking vegetables, mindless of everything but the need to place distance between themselves and their nightmare.

Eventually Fire*Wolf abandoned the road, too sickened by all he had seen to endure more of the horror, and took to the high ground. Although prompted by emotional necessity, it did in fact shorten his journey.

Fire*Wolf surveys the smoking ruins of Belgardium

By the rising of the second sun at noon, he was on a lonely hillock, silhouetted like a sentinel of doom upon his black mount, staring down on a sight which tore his soul despite the mental preparation of his meeting with the refugees.

Beneath him lay the once proud city of Belgardium. Largest port and second largest population centre in the entire realm, as the slavers had told him during his captivity. He had not known Belgardium, but it took no more than a passing glance to convince him that it was – or had been – well sited, well fortified for defence. On one side it was guarded by the Tranquil Sea; on the other by the high hills which he himself had climbed. The approaches were open and easy for the trading caravans which must have formed the city's lifeblood, but there were areas where the passes narrowed, effectively slowing the approach of any army. The fortifications, while discreet, were superbly placed: forts dotted hither and yon in strategic locations and a wall so well built of massive stone that it seemed it must endure throughout eternity.

Yet within that wall – which still stood, apparently unbreached, apparently undamaged – the city lay a smoking ruin, building after building razed to rubble as if some monstrous giant had swept a huge hand through a toy town. Only towards the seaboard did any structures remain; and even these were pitifully few.

From this distance, Fire*Wolf felt he was staring at a massive funeral pyre. He could almost smell the stench of roasting corpses. All gates lay open and through them poured the blind, the wounded, the frightened, the desperate, seeking relief in flight to

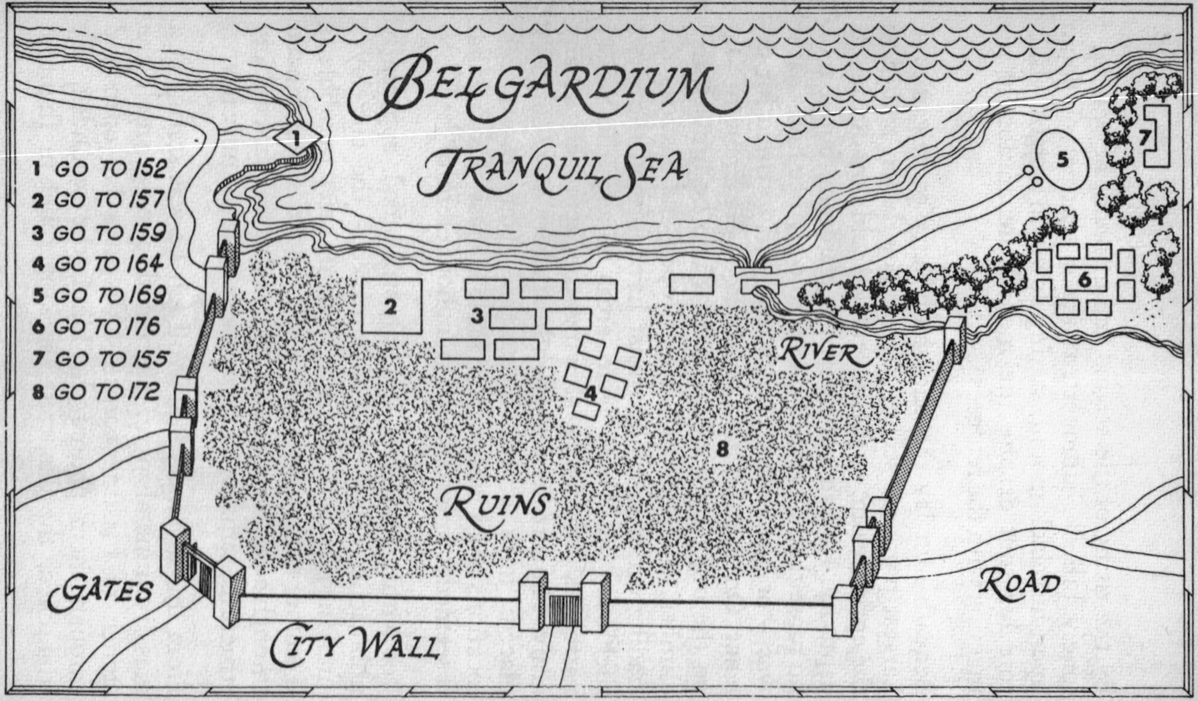
BELGARDIUM
TRANQUIL SEA
1 GO TO 152
2 GO TO 157
3 GO TO 159
4 GO TO 164
5 GO TO 169
6 GO TO 176
7 GO TO 155
8 GO TO 172
RIVER
RUINS
GATES
CITY WALL
ROAD
1
2
3
4
5
6
7
8

gods knew where. The battle – if it had been a battle – was now over. There was no indication of an enemy, no sight nor sign of the demonic Spawn. Something had attacked in darkness and laid waste to a vast urban area, then retreated, disappeared, as suddenly as it had come, leaving only horror and desolation in its wake.

There were survivors aplenty – far too many of them if the truth be told, for death would have been more merciful than the fate of these blinded and diseased inhabitants. No wonder the Lord Xandine had stressed the gravity and urgency of the situation. If this was the nature of the Demonspawn, they were the greatest blight on the face of the planet that it was possible to imagine.

Was Baldar's daughter still in this stricken city? Or was she dead or fled with the streams of refugees? He had no means of telling, but he had given his word to the hermit that he would seek the girl in Belgardium and he meant at least to try before he turned the might of his new-found sorcery against the creatures, and their masters, who had wrought this mindless, terrifying destruction.

Grimly, Fire*Wolf wheeled his horse and began to make his way downwards to the dying city.

*And here you must take a slightly different course. For it is no longer possible to chronicle Fire*Wolf's immediate destiny in any genuinely sequential manner. Opposite you will find a plan of Belgardium – or what is left of Belgardium. This is the ruined city Fire*Wolf entered and you must use it to decide what areas he chooses to visit. Be assured that while the Demonspawn seem to have* *withdrawn, there may still be substantial dangers here. But be assured too that our hero will follow his geist to success or death. The key attached to the plan will direct your steps to the relevant sections once you have made your decision about his movements.*

147

Sickened, Fire*Wolf moved out of the room and down the stairs.

As he reached the first landing, he realized his mistake. The entire slaver band and their landlord ally were in the room below.

Quickly he tried to start back, but one of them spotted him and raised the alarm. In a moment, he was fighting for his life.

*And little chance he has. There are eight slavers and the landlord. Their stats are on Page 249. You may not even wish to calculate the outcome. If you do and Fire*Wolf miraculously wins, go to* **136**. *If he dies, go to* **13**.

148

The lid of the fifth chest flew open and Fire*Wolf was momentarily blinded by the emergence of a gigantic ball of lightning which shattered all before it as it rolled inexorably towards him.

He tried to dodge, but the fiery ball changed course with him. . .

And struck!

Go to **13**.

149

Fire∗Wolf stared down at the bodies with revulsion and disdain. But he could not afford to linger. Who knew what the noise of the fight might bring down upon his head?

Swiftly he raced to the stables and released the bolts, calling urgently to those within. Startled sounds emerged, followed quickly by the first appearance of the slavers' captives, moving uncertainly, then with joy as they realized what had happened.

'Use their horses!' Fire∗Wolf called, indicating the remaining stables.

But he did not wait to see if his injunction was obeyed. He had pressing matters ahead and the road to Belgardium lay waiting.

And to reach that road, ride with Fire∗Wolf now to **135**.

150

The oak door closed behind him with a sound like the first great crack of doom. Fire∗Wolf had expected darkness, but the stone staircase was dimly illuminated by some leprous, hidden light. As he descended, the light level actually increased, taking on a greenish hue until he reached a large, circular chamber with five exits. In the centre of the chamber was a large stone statue of an old man, bearded, half crouched, dressed in ragged robes and hand outstretched – the representation of a market beggar.

Fire∗Wolf approached the statue cautiously, well aware that in this place he could not afford to take a single chance, nor assume anything was what it appeared to be. But the statue was simply stone, although close up he saw that imbedded in the outstretched palm was a glowing, pale blue crystal of a type he had never seen before.

Fire*Wolf stared at it in a long moment of indecision.

> *And already his first choice has arrived. Should he attempt to take the glowing crystal, or simply ignore it? If you feel the crystal may be useful and that he should try to take it, go to* **125**. *If not, go to* **121**.

151

Fire*Wolf began to run after the priest he had stopped, then changed his mind. The man was almost beyond rational speech as, it seemed, must be the majority of these people. Thus he waited, his eyes searching the throng in the faint hope of finding one strong heart who might be less affected by the horror than the others.

And eventually the hope was justified. Something about the walk of one – a woman in her thirties, sightless as the rest, ragged, hair matted and face covered in dried blood – suggested she might have withstood the agony a little better than the rest.

So she had. Some spark of survival instinct caused her to draw a dagger at his voice and only her blindness, and his own quick reflexes, prevented an unpleasant wound. But though she was willing enough to talk when she realized Fire*Wolf was no enemy, there was little she could tell him.

The city had been attacked by night, without warning. The first the citizens of Belgardium had known about it was when the destruction started. Afterwards it was learned that every man in the outlying forts was dead; but how they were killed, no one knew. Blindness was endemic, caused at a sweep by some sorcery applied by the Spawn. So too was disease, a wasting symptom much like leprosy, but almost instantaneous in its manifestation. This ill might well have destroyed the population as the Spawn had destroyed most of the city's buildings, had not so very many proved immune. But there was no immunity to the blindness, nor to the savage rending of the demon claws. All had been nightmare, confusion. And she knew nothing of anyone named Yalena.

After an hour spent questioning those in the great horde of refugees who could still answer him, Fire*Wolf finally admitted defeat. To hope to find news of a single woman from a vast city amongst such as these was to hope for the impossible. If he were to keep his word to Baldar, he must proceed to the city itself: without hope, admittedly, but with determination to do all he could to fulfil his pledge.

Besides, an errant whisper in his mind reminded him, the city was where he might find some useful clues to the nature of the Spawn.

*Thus was the decision made for Fire*Wolf by force of circumstance. Go with him now to Belgardium and* **146**.

152

The road branched, its main route leading to the city gates, a minor offshoot driving straight across the promontory. Fire*Wolf urged his stallion forward with caution and kept one hand within easy reaching distance of the Doomsword. At times like these, only a fool proceeded without caution.

He was approaching a Lighttower, a building which must have been of considerable importance to Belgardium before the city had been destroyed. It had obviously served a twin purpose of warning ships away from the rocks below and guiding them into the safe harbour of Belgardium itself.

It would, of course, be useless now. Belgardium was no more. Only a remnant remained, mute token to the awesome power of the Demonspawn. But if the Lighttower had been spared, perhaps those who tended it had also survived and might furnish him with important information. The difficulty would be to convince them he was not an enemy. Having witnessed the destruction of their city, they must now be ready to see agents of the Spawn everywhere.

As he came within earshot of the tower, he reined in his mount and hailed the inhabitants loudly.

There was no reply.

Cautiously, Fire*Wolf rode closer. The building was solidly made in stone, set into the bedrock of the cliff face, and gave no indication of Demonspawn attack. But nor did it give indication of anyone within. There were no guards and the entrance door was only partly closed. No light shone from the summit of the tower, but this was only to be expected during daylight hours.

Fire*Wolf called again without result, then dismounted and tethered his horse. He moved towards the door, pushed it open with the hilt of the Doomsword and peered cautiously inside.

The interior was dingy, its walls hung with ropes, buoys and other nautical equipment. A stone-built, open spiral staircase led upwards to the tower and downwards into what must be some form of basement hollowed from the bedrock.

Fire*Wolf called a third time and his voice reverberated hollowly in the confined space.

But what should he do? He has three options. He may climb the spiral staircase and explore the upper regions, in which case go to **160**. *He may descend on the same staircase in order to explore the basement, in which case turn to* **178**. *Or he may, of course, decide he is simply wasting time here, in which case return to your Key and choose another section.*

153

Cursing, Fire*Wolf flung himself full length as a second shaft hissed by his ear. The bolt in his shoulder hurt abominably, but there was no time now to remove it, so he simply snapped the flight and set his mind to ignoring the pain.

As near as he could judge, the arrows were coming from one of the small houses he had not yet investigated. Carefully he crawled forward on his belly until he judged he was hidden from the window the archer must have used. Then he rose to his feet, drew the Doomsword and leaped for the door.

It crashed inwards on the impact of his muscular frame and he had a momentary impression of round eyes and a startled expression as his assailant turned from the window, a third shaft already notched. It was a young boy, scarcely more than fourteen years of age.

In Fire*Wolf's hand, the Doomsword howled for blood.

*But should the Doomsword have its way? Should Fire*Wolf attack this young boy? And if he does not, will the youth not loose the arrow at his heart? If Fire*Wolf attacks, go to* **171**. *If not, go to* **179**.

154

The luminosity increased as Fire*Wolf approached, until, as he neared the entrance, he was enveloped in a bright green glow.

At his side, the Doomsword hummed and sang in its familiar anticipation of life essence.

Fire*Wolf was torn. His every instinct told him the greenship was empty, devoid of life or guards. And yet those same instincts warned him he was in horrendous danger – more danger, perhaps, than he had ever faced before.

And shall we not give our hero a final opportunity to take a different path?

If he proceeds into the greenship, go to **182**. *If he heeds the instinctive warning of his danger, he may go into the Temple at* **173** *– or even return to the Key to explore some other section altogether!*

155

The forest closed around him like a womb and for a time he wondered if he had lost his way. But the Wilderness sense held true and he emerged eventually into the clearing.

Close at hand, he could now tell the building was the ruin of an ancient monastery, a building old before Belgardium itself was built, the huge stone blocks of its crumbled walls mute tribute to the engineering skills or sorceries of some long dead race.

Why he had come here he did not know, but he was drawn to enter the roofless ruin and stare in wonder at the remnants of rooms too large for humankind.

He might have finished his exploration quickly were it not for the radiant unease of the Doomsword at his side. Fire*Wolf touched the blade briefly and at once the smooth voice sounded within his mind:

'Brave Barbarian, we must leave this place!'

'Why?' asked Fire*Wolf mentally, intrigued by the hint of panic in the demon voice.

'There is power beneath the ground. It pains me.'

*Power beneath the ground? Should Fire*Wolf explore further? If so, go to* **165**. *Or should he take the advice of his sword and leave? If so, return to the Key and choose another area.*

156

The corridor ran due south and carried Fire*Wolf directly to a closed, but unlocked doorway. Unlocked, that is, until he entered, when bolts automatically

slammed in place behind him, sealing his escape.
He was in a great hall, empty except for a transparent crystal box set into the middle of the floor. There was no discernible exit, but within the box, Fire*Wolf could clearly see the outlines of a level – and a glittering golden coin. A brass plaque set into the stonework before the crystal box carried the following message:

READ INSTRUCTIONS CAREFULLY

Unless the word and is used in the spelling of Xandine, scratch a circle on the floor, otherwise make that a square, except where the square root of 49 is less than 8 in which case add a line through whichever shape you drew in the first place and tap the crystal box the number of times represented by the letter G where A is 1 and finally, assuming C is three stamp whichever of your feet is represented by sixty-two a number of times equivalent to J+M on top of the box unless you can discover a single figure odd number which becomes an even number after you turn it upside down in which case subtract the even number from J+M and stamp that number of times, unless you drew a line through the figure you scratched in which case add the number to J+M and stamp that number plus 2.

*Dear gods, could Fire*Wolf cope with that at all? Did he draw a square? Did he draw a circle? Did he scratch a line through it? And how many times did he knock? And how many times did he stamp? And which stupid foot did he use? Take your pick!*

Drew	With line	Foot	Knocked	Stamped	Go To
Square	Yes	Right	7	31	**161**
Square	No	Right	7	17	**168**
Square	No	Left	7	17	**177**
Circle	No	Right	7	17	**126**
Circle	Yes	Right	7	31	**158**
Committed suicide					**13**

157

The building, he quickly discovered, was a fort – and a well-run fort from every indication. It had apparently been established to keep order in the dockland district and staffed with soldiers trained to deal with trouble efficiently and swiftly. But though the structure was sound, with no indication whatsoever of attack or any other form of violence, the fort was empty.

Walking through the empty chambers, Fire*Wolf experienced the nervous apprehension of a man trapped in a haunted house. There were signs of habitation everywhere – a late supper for twenty men half-eaten on a dining table; lighted lamps, their wicks well trimmed; scrolls showing a ship's manifest, neatly laid out on a desk; bunks with bedclothes turned back as if the sleepers had but recently awakened . . . all the signs of people without the people themselves. For while he searched diligently, he could not find a living soul.

In a way this building was even more disturbing than the ruinous destruction of the remainder of the city. Had the warriors awakened and rushed out to fight the

Spawn? It was possible, yet their weapons remained in the armoury. Had the Spawn entered silently to murder every one? That too was possible, but then where were the corpses?

In one room, Fire*Wolf found a half-written letter which he read with the difficulty of one brought up in the Wilderness. It was a love letter from a soldier to his wife, living, it seemed, in a village some distance from Belgardium. The words were gentle, carrying no hint of danger; yet the letter ended in mid-sentence, as if the writer had been suddenly disturbed.

Depressed, Fire*Wolf left the building.

Return to the Key and choose another area to explore.

158

The box explodes. Go to **13**.

159

The buildings were huge. They towered above Fire*Wolf undisturbed by the attacks of the Spawn as if they were prepared to stand like grubby sentinels for an eternity.

The doorways were enormous, barred, locked but now unguarded. Fire*Wolf stopped by a convenient window-slit in the nearest of the buildings and peered inside. If he had not already guessed it, even a passing glimpse confirmed that these were the great coastal warehouses of Belgardium, packed with the cargoes of a thousand ships.

What riches were here for the taking! Yet the Spawn had not taken them, had totally ignored them in fact.

160

Moving from one warehouse to another, Fire*Wolf quickly satisfied himself that none had been disturbed, although in two of them, he found dead guards collapsed at their posts near the doors. How the men had died was impossible to say, for there was no obvious wound or mark. But they had died in horror to judge from the expressions on their faces.

He tried each door in turn and found each perfectly secure. So far as he could tell, no window or shutter had been broken either. The entire dockland, once the bustling hub of trade and transport, was now utterly deserted. Whatever he had hoped to find, he would not find it here.

Return to your Key and investigate another area.

160

He emerged eventually on to an open battlement which commanded a clear view of the ruined city and the Tranquil Sea. The two lay in stark contrast before his troubled gaze, so that after only moments, he found an open doorway to the huge lantern chamber and went inside gratefully.

The chamber was a marvel of sophisticated engineering and Fire*Wolf's Barbarian soul was briefly in awe of the linked banks of lanterns and their communal reservoir of oil deep enough to drown a dozen men. His eyes swept across the complex of interlinking cogs and levers which drove the massive shutters around the lamps themselves.

But for all its marvellous machinery, for all the indications that the tower had been well tended, there were no people here. He might have left then, had his eye not fallen on an open journal resting beside a quill and inks on a small table near the door. He picked it up and began to read with the studious concentration of a Barbarian ill-versed in arts divorced from combat.

But for all his difficulty, he realized swiftly enough that he had found a prize. For the journal was a written record of the Demonspawn attack.

It had been utterly unexpected. In the spring, the State astrologers had forewarned of the coming of the Spawn, but the experience of centuries confirmed that safety was assured until the snows melted in the mountain passes. Thus life went on for a time with the nervous appearance of normality – although the journal remarked that many of the Kingdom's rich and powerful families had taken ship in face of the threat. For the common people, no such luxury was possible and life went on in the desperate hope that the Ruling Council might somehow halt the Spawn; and in the certain expectation that if doomsday lay around the corner, there was at least a little time before the corner need be turned.

Yet with the passes blocked, the Spawn had come to raze Belgardium. The writer of the journal was evidently a keeper of the Lighttower's lamps. He had been awake and alert when the leprous luminescence of the Spawn greenships had appeared in the night sky above Belgardium's protecting hills. Wave after wave had come in the eerie silence of a nightmare, breaking ranks only briefly as some of their number settled on the outlying forts while the remainder swooped with slow deliberation on the city itself.

There had been no time to raise an alarm, no time to escape, no time for anything but observation. . .

Fire*Wolf set down the journal, sickened. The vivid description of what happened next sent waves of nausea rolling from his stomach to settle in his throat. But with the nausea came anger, a fury at these creatures who played god with human life. If ever he had had a doubt about the mantle placed upon his shoulders by Lord Xandine, that doubt was now resolved. No task held greater urgency, greater importance, than the extermination of these vermin.

He was on the point of turning away when a final entry caught his eye. With the city in ruins, its inhabitants dead, dying, blinded or diseased, the greenships had taken off in precision formation and flown away northwards; all but one. One remained. While the writer did not know why, he did know where. The greenship remained somewhere near the great Temple of Belgardium.

With a glint of grim determination in his eyes, Fire*Wolf left the Lighttower and remounted his horse.

*Return to the Key and choose Fire*Wolf's next area to explore.*

161

*The box opens, permitting Fire*Wolf to take the coin and pull the lever which opens up a secret exit. Go to* **180**.

162

Go to **125**.

163

His head high, Fire*Wolf snapped brusquely to the landlord, 'A bed for the night and a stable for my horse!'

'Of course, good sir. Of course.' The landlord bustled obsequiously, his eyes evaluating the worth of Fire*Wolf's robe.

But Fire*Wolf ignored him and walked directly to the doorway, brushing past Tojar as if he were a serf. The slaver stared at him with a puzzled frown, but made no move to stop him, nor gave any real sign of recognition.

A wave of heat struck Fire*Wolf as he walked into the tavern proper. It was a busy scene. Serving wenches scurried with jugs of ale and plates of food to scrubbed pine tables in a room well filled with customers. These were merchants mainly, with a scattering of soldiers, some florid, quiet men who might have been local farmers and, in a group in one corner, virtually the entire slaver band. But where were their charges? Where were the slaves?

No one paid the slightest attention as Fire*Wolf pushed towards an empty table in a secluded corner well away from the slaver band. Although he seemed to have passed by Tojar without recognition, he had no wish to press his luck. He had, after all, killed one of their number and while he was, in looks, a far cry from the half-naked Barbarian they had captured, he was under no illusions as to the outcome if they recognised him.

A young girl of no more than sixteen appeared beside him, dressed in the apron and kirtle of a serving wench.

'Bring me ale,' Fire*Wolf told her, 'and food. Then prepare me a room for the night.'

'Yes, sir.'

As he ate, he watched the slaver party from the corner of his eye. They were drinking heavily, growing noisy and soon, it seemed, were destined to lapse into a stupor. Fire*Wolf caught the eye of the girl who had served him. When she returned to his table, he asked quietly, 'Those men in the corner – who are they?'

'Northerners,' the girl said shortly. Young though she was, she seemed intelligent. The expression on her face suggested she was less than enamoured with the bearded men.

'Merchants?'

She shook her head, but then added, 'Of a sort. They trade in human merchandise.' She stared at Fire*Wolf. 'Are they friends of yours?'

He shrugged. 'I engage in different trade.' He was about to ask more questions when the girl was called away.

By the time he had finished his meal, the landlord reappeared to tell him that his room was ready. Fire*Wolf went to it directly. It was small, but clean and the bed looked more inviting than anything he had seen in months. He undressed quickly, left the Doomsword within reach beside the bed and fell almost at once into an exhausted, dreamless sleep.

He awoke to a startled gasp, the Doomsword in his hand. The room was dark, but moonlight streaming through the window illuminated the frightened face of the serving girl bent over him, the gently singing tip of the Doomsword at her throat.

Fire*Wolf controlled the blade with an effort. Its lust for blood was growing stronger, as was its power. Had he taken only moments longer to awaken, it would have drunk of the girl's soul using his unconscious hand. He set the sword down and stared at the frightened girl. 'What are you doing in my room?' he asked softly, but with an anger that was partly directed towards himself.

She swallowed. 'I came to warn you.'

Fire*Wolf sat up. 'Warn me?'

'The men you asked me about – the Northerners who trade slaves. They know you. I think they plan to kill you.'

'So!' Fire*Wolf said. He swung his feet out of bed and reached for his robe. The girl's eyes widened at the rippling musculature of his body, but he ignored her. As he dressed, he asked, 'Do you know when?'

'Tonight. That's why I came to warn you. My father has agreed to the plan because they promised him your gold, so there is no one to aid you.'

'Your father?'

'The landlord.'

Fire*Wolf nodded, abruptly noting hints of a family resemblance.

'What are you going to do?' she asked.

Fire*Wolf did not answer. He was considering two possibilities.

*One possibility is flight, and the obvious one at that. With the girl to help him, there is no doubt that Fire*Wolf can make good his escape. But the other route, in keeping with his deepest instincts, is to fight. Sorcery, if he can bring himself to use it, would make him a match for the whole slaver band. Which decision will he reach? If he decides to flee, go to* **128**. *If he decides to fight, go to* **142**.

164

Here was the tragedy of all Belgardium in miniature. As Fire*Wolf approached, he knew immediately he had stumbled on a freak circumstance, for unique in all the ruined city, here stood a handful of artisan dwellings, totally undamaged in the attack.

But though the houses still stood, the disaster of Belgardium had overtaken their inhabitants. The first door he tried opened easily, but he halted in the doorway, stopped by the sickly sweet odour of death and disease. In the small room within lay a whole family, all dead. Their corpses clearly showed signs of the foul malady he had already seen among the refugees.

Fire*Wolf backed away, closing the door quietly behind him. It was almost as much as he could do, but he forced himself to examine the interior of another house. Here the scene was not so horrifying. Although there were three corpses, none carried the marks of disease.

He left this house too and was walking towards another when the arrow struck him in the shoulder.

And removed a double dice roll of LIFE POINTS *into the bargain. (If this kills him, go to* **13**.*) But what now? Fire*Wolf may flee, in which case you should* *return to the Key and choose another section. Or he may attempt to close with his hidden assailant, in which case turn to* **153**.

165

He left the Doomsword outside the ruin. This time, to his intense surprise, it did not reappear instantly at his side as he returned inside.

Beneath the ground, the demon of the sword had told him. But where?

After more than an hour of diligent searching, he had come to wonder if he were fooling himself. These ruins had surely been thoroughly explored by residents of and visitors to Belgardium. Could anything have been overlooked?

Just when he was about to give up and reclaim his demonic sword, something impinged itself on Fire*Wolf's attention. It was not on the ground where he had been searching, but rather on one of the ruined walls. It was a faded insignia, cut into the stone, like a mason's mark or the remnant of some ancient family crest.

The symbol was so worn as to be almost invisible except in certain lights, so that luck was certainly with Fire*Wolf in noticing it at all. But it was not the insignia itself which intrigued him so much as an imbalance within its design. He traced the imbalance with his fingers, then spun round in alarm as a slab moved, earth fell and a stairway opened at his feet.

*Should Fire*Wolf really risk entering this hidden crypt? Especially without the protection of his*

Doomsword? If you feel the answer must be yes, then turn at once to **181**. *If not, you may always return to the Key and choose another area to explore.*

166

The lid of the first chest flew open and a noxious billow of green smoke poured out to fill the room. Fire*Wolf gasped.

An unwise thing to do in a room full of virulently poisonous gas. Go to **13**.

167

The Doomsword howled in its frustration as the slim figure of a teenage girl entered the room and Fire*Wolf forced himself to hold his demon blade. The girl gasped, startled by the looming figure before her.

Unwilling to take any chances, Fire*Wolf placed the point at her throat and said quietly, 'Who are you, girl – and what are you doing here?'

She froze to stillness, but replied calmly enough, 'I am the daughter of the landlord here. I came to free you.'

'Why should you do that?' Fire*Wolf asked suspiciously. 'It was your father who struck me.'

'I do not always approve of my father's activities.' She took a deep, shuddering breath and added, 'Now, if you plan to remove my head, please do so, otherwise put down that sword.'

After a moment, Fire*Wolf lowered his weapon. The girl entered the room quickly and closed the door behind her, although he noticed she took care that it did not close completely.

'They plan to kill you this night,' she said without preamble. 'We must hurry if you are to escape.'

'They?'

'The Northerners who trade in slaves. I do not know their quarrel with you, but I do know my father must not be implicated in a murder. Will you trust me to show you the way to freedom? It is useless to try the stairs – they are in the room below. You must leave by the window.'

But it is not, in fact, merely a matter of trust. In fact Fire∗Wolf has no reason to disbelieve this girl. His indecision stems from a desire for revenge on the slavers. Should he attempt to exact it now, or should he make good his escape? If he seeks revenge, go to **133**. *If he decides to escape, go to* **128**.

168

The box explodes. Go to **13.**

169

The pathway through well-kept grounds was in stark contrast with the destruction of the city. Here was peace, as if the attack had never been. There was no indication of destruction, no sweet smell of rotting corpses or disease. Yet Fire∗Wolf was uneasy. Something nibbled at the edges of his perception as if a fog of evil lurked ready to envelop him at any moment.

At his side, the Doomsword hummed its anticipation of the combat sure to come, and come swiftly.

A noise to his right sent him swinging without thought towards a shrub bed. No more than instants later he was running with the Doomsword singing in his hand towards the creature crawling in the undergrowth.

But this was no Demonspawn, as he quickly discovered, but a wounded, white-robed young man with the tonsure of a priestly acolyte. One glance was enough to tell Fire*Wolf he was dying.

'What befell you?' he asked quickly.

The man stared up at him with pain-filled eyes. For a moment he seemed unable to speak. Then he gasped, 'The Spawn are in the Temple. Their accursed greenship lies within the sacred grounds. Their unholy Regent sits upon the Golden Throne. They . . . they . . .'

His voice faded so that Fire*Wolf was forced to bend to catch the final words.

'They hold the girl Yalena hostage as a trap for the . . . for the . . .'

Yalena! So she was here! Held hostage as a trap for – whom? The hermit's daughter had become a pawn in some larger game. The young acolyte was nearly gone, a gurgle in his throat masking his last remaining words. No matter. Destiny had presented Fire*Wolf with the opportunity to combine both his fates. He would free Yalena and strike his first blow at the Spawn.

'Where do they hold her?' he asked urgently.

'In . . . in . . . yfilclr . . .'

It was useless. The man was dead, slain by the very creatures who now defiled the Temple of Belgardium.

Fire*Wolf straightened, turned and walked back to the path.

In minutes he had reached the Temple grounds unchallenged. No guards were posted, no Spawn was in sight. The Temple itself rose up before him, a serene edifice in white marble, pure as the scudding clouds on a summer's day. And beside it, sullen as a fungoid leech, squatted the greenship, a low, saucer-like metallic vehicle, faintly luminous and silent, its entrance port open as an invitation.

*Where now? Should Fire*Wolf enter the greenship (go to* **154***) or the Temple itself (go to* **173***)? The choice is yours.*

170

The corridor ran south before branching south east. Fire*Wolf followed it with increasing impatience until, to his surprise, it opened into what he could only to be a boudoir.

In the middle of the richly carpeted floor was an ornate four-poster bed. In the bed was a woman of dark, good looks who smiled and beckoned him towards her.

Fire*Wolf stepped forward and the door of the chamber closed silently behind him.

This is, despite appearances, one of the most dangerous tests our hero will ever face. It is a test of his ATTRACTION. *Throw two dice and multiply the result by eight to find the test figure. Compare this with his* ATTRACTION *statistic. If the figure you have just thrown is lower, then the woman in the bed will make love to our hero and present him* *with a gold coin for his efforts. If the figure you have thrown is higher, the woman will still make love to him, but at the moment of satisfaction will be transformed into a gigantic Black Widow spider. Those who know the mating habits of Black Widows will not be surprised to learn this means, for poor Fire*Wolf,* **13**.

171

As Fire*Wolf swung the howling Doomsword, the boy fired – and missed. But he was fast, this youth, and managed not only to dodge the fearful blow, but also to draw a short sword of his own. Screaming, he launched himself towards Fire*Wolf.

*This fight must end in death for one of them. You will find the boy's stats on page 249. Calculate the outcome. If Fire*Wolf dies, go to* **13**. *If he survives, he will find nothing more of note here, thus go to the Key and choose another area to investigate.*

172

The violence of the destruction was almost unimaginable. It had seemed great from a distance, but now Fire*Wolf saw his earlier impression had been softened by perspective. Close at hand, he could see the toppled stonework of the great buildings, the corpse-strewn mounds of rubble, the collapsed bridges, the hanging archways, the torn roads and pavements.

What manner of creatures had the power to engage in such devastation? Like a whisper on the wind the answer came back . . . the Spawn.

But how was the destruction wrought? He saw the remains of walls which would have withstood an army of battering rams for weeks, walls which were now in ruins. He saw roadways gouged and cratered, remnants of houses that were scarcely more than dust. Everywhere he could see the dead and dying, for those who could still move were joining in the great caravans of refugees which still streamed, without relief, out of the city's open gates.

Fire*Wolf wandered for long hours amid the desolation, half hoping for some indication of Yalena, more realistically searching for clues to the nature of the Demonspawn. Everything he saw increased his horror of these monsters created by a wizard race so long ago. Their power seemed absolute. In one portion of the ruins the very stones were vitrified and fused as if subjected to great heat. In another a wall had been torn as a child might tear paper. In a third he watched fascinated while a mansion, apparently untouched, suddenly collapsed into powder when caught by a sudden gust of wind.

At length he tired of his ghoulish investigation. If Yalena remained alive, she was not here in the midst of such destruction. She could only be within the sanctuary of those buildings on the seaboard which seemed to have escaped the worst of the attack. Even there her chances of survival may well have been slim. Nonetheless, he had to look. Fire*Wolf closed his eyes to orient himself as to his whereabouts in the ruined city.

Return to the Key to Plan.

173

Like blasphemy triumphant, the scream of a woman in pain rent the air of sacred grove as Fire*Wolf approached the Temple.

He was moving openly, driven by anger, and had half expected an open attack. But no Spawn guards emerged from the Temple. Indeed, had it not been for his encounter with the dying acolyte – and now the scream – the building might have seemed deserted.

Half running, he mounted the shallow entrance steps, Doomsword unsheathed and howling its expectation as never before. This, he knew, might call for sorcery as well as sword. The Spawn were magical creatures about which he knew far too little, so no weapon against them could be unreasonably discarded.

The sanctum of the Temple was immense, created for communal worship of Belgardium's seafaring gods. Shrines to the individual deities were everywhere, but towering colonnades led the eye at once to the sanctum's central feature, the low dais with its Golden Throne, perpetually empty to receive the essence of the god when offering was made on the altar before it.

But the throne was not empty now, nor was the altar. Crouching on the throne, its eyes firmly fixed on Fire*Wolf, was a squat, green-scaled creature wearing dull green armour, stubby bat-wings enveloping its broad shoulders like a cloak. On the altar before it was a woman chained and naked, her body bruised and bleeding, her face contorted in a mask of terror.

Fire*Wolf rescues Yalena

The thing on the throne smiled. 'Welcome, Messiah. I thought my little plaything would draw you quickly to me.'

The thing was alone. No guards protected it. With a cry that matched the howling of his Doomsword, Fire*Wolf launched himself upon it.

Perhaps rashly, for while there are no guards, perhaps the Spawn Regent does not need them. Too late now, though. Turn to page 250 for details of the Regent's stats, physical and magical and calculate the outcome on the basis of the information given. If our hero survives, go to **183**. *If not, there is only* **13**.

174

The noise appeared to be coming from one of the largest crates. As Fire*Wolf approached, he could see the lid was slightly ajar. At once his Wilderness instincts were aroused, so that he drew the Doomsword and moved silent as a cat to throw the case open.

With a roar he swung the sword and twisted to look inside . . . in time to see the thin tail of a mouse disappearing through a small hole in the side.

*Something of an anticlimax, but then a hero's life is not all aggression. If Fire*Wolf has not already explored the upper region, he may do so now by moving to* **160**. *Alternatively, he may wish to return to the Key and explore another area.*

175

The lid of the second chest flew open. Fire*Wolf approached it cautiously. Inside lay a single glittering golden coin.

*And with this coin in his possession, Fire*Wolf will now discover the exit door of the chamber opens easily. Go to* **180**.

176

The forest path widened abruptly, opening on to close-cropped lawns. In the centre was a low, but pleasing structure mainly built in pink-veined granite and surrounded by a collection of smaller buildings of the same general design and construction. Moving warily, Fire*Wolf entered the nearest of them to discover it was a communal dormitory . . . and empty.

In less than an hour, he had explored the entire complex thoroughly. What he found made two things obvious: it was here that the priests of the Temple made their residence and not one priest remained within the area. Nor was there the slightest indication of their fate.

Return to the Key and choose another area to explore.

177

The box explodes. Go to **13**.

178

The stairway rose in a spiral a short distance to leave him in what was obviously a storage room. Near the bottom of the stairwell were sacks of foodstuffs. The remainder of the chamber was cluttered with crates, packing cases and equipment similar to that hanging on the walls above. There was even a small wooden dinghy set on chocks near the far wall.

'Hello?' Fire*Wolf called.

In the silence that followed he thought he heard a sound. Frowning, he stepped forward, then stopped.

Stopped in indecision. The sound was small, almost certainly a mouse. Should he investigate? If there was anyone in the Lighttower, he had no wish to persuade them he was a thief, as they might do if they discovered him rummaging through the basement. So his choice is simple: investigate the noise and go to **174***; ignore it and explore the upper regions by going to* **160** *(or, if he has already explored the upper regions, he may return to the Key to investigate another area altogether).*

179

Fire*Wolf hesitated.

The youthful archer hesitated.

For an instant that stretched into an eternity, they stared at one another, the huge Barbarian with his howling Doomsword, the slim youth with his deadly bow. Then the boy dropped the weapon and sank sobbing to the floor. 'Not Spawn,' he murmured to himself again and again. 'Not Spawn. Not Spawn. Not Spawn.'

Fire*Wolf sheathed the reluctant Doomsword and waited awkwardly. 'What happened?' he asked when, eventually, the boy's emotions came under some control.

'They killed my parents,' the boy said softly. 'They destroyed the city. They have left their Regent in the Holy Temple. They – '

179

'A moment, 'Fire*Wolf said quickly. 'You say their Regent remains?'

'At the Temple,' the boy nodded, 'with my step-sister.'

'Your step-sister?' Fire*Wolf echoed. He felt at once bewildered and excited. If a Demonspawn Regent remained, here surely was a chance to strike back in some small measure. Here surely was an opportunity to exact some small revenge. But how had this boy's relative become involved?

'There is something they fear,' the boy said. 'For all their power, there is something they fear. They have taken her to bait a trap.'

It grew more and more confusing. But Fire*Wolf clung to that central thought of vengeance. 'Make good your escape,' he told the boy abruptly and turned to go.

'Where are you going, Warrior?' the boy cried.

'To the Temple,' said Fire*Wolf grimly. 'To execute some murderers.'

'Warrior, will you save my step-sister?'

Fire*Wolf glanced at him. 'If it is in my power. What is her name?'

'Yalena,' the boy said. 'Her name is Yalena.'

> *So it seems that Destiny has turned full circle. If Fire*Wolf goes directly to the Temple, turn to* **169**. *If there are other areas you feel he should first explore, return to the Key and make your choice.*

180

The corridor ran downwards then rose in a confusion of levels until Fire*Wolf finally faced a closed door. Cautiously he tried the handle and, to his surprise, found it opened easily.

He stepped through and found himself standing half way down a flight of familiar steps. The door itself closed quietly behind him and blended so perfectly with the stonework as to become invisible.

Fire*Wolf started downwards, convinced he knew where the staircase was leading. And he was right. Moments later, he had stepped out into the chamber with the beggar's statue.

Half running in his excitement, he deposited the gold coin on the outstretched hand, taking care not to touch the glowing crystal directly. At once the coin vanished in a flash of pale blue light.

The statue spoke!

'You have paid my fee, Adventurer,' it intoned in a voice that suggested some mechanical contrivance. 'Thus is the magic nullified and you may leave by any exit in the knowledge that it will carry you safely beyond this place. But first I must speak to you of POWER.

'The coin you have donated has accumulated for you no more than twenty points of POWER. If this gives you sufficient for your goals, then leave now with my blessing. But if you wish to accumulate more POWER then the Ordeal must continue. So choose now, Adventurer – exit or Ordeal!'

*Some choice! If Fire*Wolf decides to leave the Crypts*

with the POWER *he has accumulated, then go to* **122**. *If not, then he may simply choose Ordeal and pick one of the standard exits – 1 =* **129**: *2 =* **137**: *3 =* **145**: *4 =* **156**: *5 =* **170**. *But bear in mind, the magic of the Crypts will not permit him to visit any section he has previously entered.*

181

He descended into a stone lined burial chamber, musty with age, cobwebbed and bright.

Bright?

There was a light source in the chamber!

Fire*Wolf's startled eyes took in the granite sarcophagus, the corpse it may have housed once long since mouldered into dust. But within the sarcophagus, as if it had been placed on the breast of a dead king, lay a glowing orb.

And even Fire*Wolf's earthy soul could not help but sense the magical aura which surrounded it.

*Should Fire*Wolf take the orb? To do so he will risk his very life, as you may well have guessed. Until he touches the orb, he may not know its nature. But to touch the orb will require you to make a check roll against his* LUCK. *Two dice multiplied by eight and if the result is higher than his natural* LUCK *figure, then he dies. (Go to* **13**). *He may ignore the orb completely, returning to the Key and seeking out another area to explore. Or he may take the risk. If he succeeds, you will find a description of the orb on page 250.*

The light became a fog and out of the fog came a creature.

There could be no friends here. Fire*Wolf drew the Doomsword and leaped forward. But the blade twisted in his hand as if it had a life of its own and plunged with savage fury into his own breast.

'I am called by my kin, Barbarian,' the suave voice of Lucifuge Rofocal echoed in his mind.

Go to **13**.

183

Fire*Wolf released the sobbing girl and held her to his breast. The body of the Spawn Regent was already an oozing pool of putrefaction, as if death had abruptly severed the sorcerous threads which held its physical form together.

'Fear not, Yalena,' Fire*Wolf murmured kindly. 'I have news of Baldar your father, and the thing which held you is now dead.'

It was as if she had not heard him. 'The Regent is dead,' she sobbed. 'Only the Regent. The Spawn remain. . .'

Indeed this was true enough. The hard-won victory stood for nothing in the greater game. If the battle had been worth recording, it was only because this was his first encounter with the Spawn. But small or not, it was still victory and, for the moment, he savoured it. Tomorrow would be time enough to plan his future actions.

Although one thing puzzled him sufficiently to detract, at least a little, from the joy of battle won. The

183

creature had called him 'Messiah' and hinted it had trapped him into coming.

Now what, Fire*Wolf wondered, had the Spawn Regent meant by that?

*Here ends Book One of the Sagas of the Demonspawn. Follow Fire*Wolf's further adventures in Book Two: 'The Crypts of Terror.'*

SPECIAL SECTION A

FIRE*WOLF THE SORCERER

If your character has got this far – especially with a decent POWER reserve – you certainly deserve congratulation. The chances now are excellent that he will complete the first phase of his epic adventure without getting killed too often.

For now Fire*Wolf is no longer a mere fighting man, but is, at least potentially, a sorcerer as well.

In a moment, we'll go into exactly what that means. Meanwhile, a subtle but important point:

You know Fire*Wolf abhors sorcery. He has been forced by circumstances to equip himself as a practitioner of the Mystic Arts: but how far will his horror of things magical permit him to use them? He is already, as you know, extremely upset by the Doomsword, although sheer survival has forced him to use it frequently. Will he really begin with wild abandon to throw fireballs at every foe he meets simply because he has the POWER and Art to do so?

The answer is, of course, that he will not. However desperate the situation, there is still a strong chance his natural inclinations will get the upper hand and force him to ignore his sorcerous powers in favour of his strong right arm.

Thus, there will henceforth be certain rules you must follow in Fire*Wolf's application of the Mystic Arts. The rules are these:

1. Before Fire*Wolf can use any spell, you must make a check roll to determine his natural inclination. Roll two dice. If our hero fails to score 4 or better on the roll, *he will not use* ANY *sorcery in the current section, however hard pressed he may be.*
2. However much POWER he has at his disposal, he will *never use the same spell twice in a single section.* (He may, of course, use different spells in the same section if he has the POWER to do so.)

Alongside this, it must be remembered that, as King Arthur's Druid Wizard Merlin used to say, sorcery is not a bowl of cherries. Thus, while a spell may be cast, it will not always work. It is in the nature of the Mystic Arts that they include an automatic *Fundamental Failure Rate* (FFR for short).

The FFR of sorcery means that each time a spell is cast, our hero must throw 6 or better on two dice to determine whether or not the spell succeeds.

The annoying thing about this is that a spell requires POWER to cast, not to work. So even if the dice roll shows the spell has failed, the POWER applied in casting it is still used up.

Spell Power

In the list which follows, POWER expenditure is shown for each spell. Unless Fire*Wolf has sufficient POWER at the time he wishes to cast a spell, he simply cannot do so. The best he can do is decide to use that spell in a future section if POWER becomes available to him.

This means, in effect, that Fire*Wolf has two chances to beat his natural inclinations. The first chance comes when he has insufficient POWER to cast a particular spell. At that time you can make a check roll on his natural inclination – and even if it goes against the grain, you can make a second check in a new section when POWER becomes available. If the second check is favourable, then he can use the spell.

Power Renewal

Fire*Wolf's experiences in the Crypts have given him a new statistic – his POWER figure. This now becomes as much a part of his character as his SPEED, STRENGTH, SKILL etc. stats.

But unlike the others, POWER is dispersed each time a spell is cast. For Fire*Wolf to survive his adventures, there must be some way in which his POWER can be regained.

In point of fact, there are three possibilities open to him in this respect:

1. He can simply take a chance and carry on his adventure. In every new Section he enters, he will automatically regain 1 POWER point. This is regained POWER only: it cannot ever take him beyond his original POWER total.
2. He may trade off his LIFE POINTS for POWER on a one for one basis. That is to say, if he wishes to use a

spell and does not have the POWER available, he may elect to use one LIFE POINT to replace each point of POWER needed.

3. He may make use (providing he has reserved sufficient POWER) of the Crypt Spell, which will not alone give him an opportunity to regain POWER but is actually his only certain means of increasing his POWER stat.

SPELL TABLE

SPELL	EFFECT	POWER
ARMOUR	Creates a magical armour of light around Fire*Wolf for the duration of the section. This subtracts 10 points from any damage scored against him in combat.	25
CRYPT	Returns Fire*Wolf to **150** from where he may take as many of the tests as he wishes in order to restore or increase his POWER.	10
FIREBALL	Hurls a magical ball of flame from Fire*Wolf's palm which, if the spell succeeds, will cause 50 LIFE POINTS damage to an enemy.	15
INVISIBILITY	Renders Fire*Wolf invisible for the remainder of the section. He cannot attack an enemy while invisible, but he can avoid combat and proceed to the following section as if he had been the victor.	30

PARALYSIS	Causes the total paralysis of a single enemy for sufficient time to allow Fire*Wolf to escape to the next section.	30
POISON NEEDLE	Shoots a poisoned needle from Fire*Wolf's finger into any single enemy within combat range. This needle is invariably fatal to the enemy of whatever size if the spell works, providing the enemy is not naturally immune. Check immunity with a single die roll. A score above 3 shows the poison will not work.	25
RESURRECTION	The only known way to avoid the dreaded **13**. When this spell succeeds, it will return Fire*Wolf to the start of the current section. Any enemy he has been fighting will retain only the LIFE POINTS he had when Fire*Wolf died. Completely new stats will, however, have to be rolled for Fire*Wolf himself. This spell may ONLY be used when Fire*Wolf is killed.	50

RETRACE	Allows Fire*Wolf to return to any section he has previously visited and to proceed with his adventure from there. Note that his LIFE POINTS or POWER are not restored.	20
TIMEWARP	Causes Time to return to the beginning of the current section. This spell is generally used in combat since it has the effect of restoring Fire*Wolf's LIFE POINTS to where they were at that point. Unfortunately his opponent's LIFE POINTS are similarly restored.	10
XENOPHOBIA	Causes a single opponent to feel such fear of Fire*Wolf that he (the enemy) fights at a disadvantage so that 5 points are automatically subtracted from any damage scored against Fire*Wolf.	15

FIGHTING STATISTICS

	BALDAR	BANDIT	CONSTRICTOR LIZARD	TIGON
STRENGTH	48	50	96	90
SPEED	36	48	20	80
STAMINA	90	48	55	75
COURAGE	90	40	80	85
SKILL	44	20	25	22
LUCK	48	30	16	16
CHARM	40	16	2	9
ATTRACTION	16	20	0	5
LIFE POINTS:	412	272	294	382

	BAJ	PAN-THERINE	GREAT-HOUND	ARCANA
STRENGTH	60	88	58	58
SPEED	50	96	55	60
STAMINA	48	50	45	60
COURAGE	55	80	70	80
SKILL	16	25	15	33
LUCK	40	40	10	60
CHARM	20	10	15	80
ATTRACTION	25	5	0	95
LIFE POINTS:	314	394	268	526

	DEMON	OLD WOMAN	GIANT SPIDER	YVEEN
STRENGTH	150	82	90	65
SPEED	100	44	70	60
STAMINA	100	50	45	48
COURAGE	120	60	70	66
SKILL	70	16	30	20
LUCK	100	48	30	65
CHARM	0	25	0	80
ATTRACTION	0	16	0	95
LIFE POINTS:	640	341	335	499

	TOJAR	ARCHER	LANDLORD	NORTHERN SLAVER
STRENGTH	75	55	55	60
SPEED	50	65	30	55
STAMINA	48	35	65	50
COURAGE	55	85	45	40
SKILL	10	6	45	40
LUCK	50	55	40	30
CHARM	16	55	50	8
ATTRACTION	50	55	45	30
LIFE POINTS:	354	411	335	283

ILLUSION LIZARD

Special stats in that it will take on whatever strength etc. its current enemy imagines.
LIFE POINTS are 384 Roll for Fire*Wolf's conception of its STRENGTH and STAMINA.

DOOMBRINGER

Technically, the sword has stats similar to the Demon (above). In practice these are irrelevant to its fighting abilities. Each time it is used to strike a blow, the blade will absorb 10 of Fire*Wolf's LIFE POINTS (and may kill him in the process) but if the blow is successful Doombringer absorbs the LIFE POINTS deducted from the enemy and transfers them directly to Fire*Wolf up to his legal maximum. The sword strikes with a force of +20 (i.e. 10 above that of a normal blade).

THE ORB

The Orb is a remarkable find indeed. It is an ancient magical artifact created as a weapon against the Demonspawn. It may be used in one of two ways. Held in the left hand during combat, it will DOUBLE any damage scored against a member of the Spawn race. Hurled at a Demonspawn, it will explode on contact, killing the Spawn instantly. But this, of course, destroys the Orb. There is also a small chance of missing when the Orb is thrown: it requires a roll of 4 or better on double dice to ensure a hit. However, even a miss will damage a Spawn to the extent of 200 LIFE POINTS which may well kill it in any case.

THE DEMONSPAWN REGENT

STRENGTH	150
SPEED	110
STAMINA	100
COURAGE	150
SKILL	100
LUCK	0
CHARM	0
ATTRACTION	0
LIFE POINTS	610

Less LIFE POINTS, perhaps, than you might have imagined—although nothing to be sneezed at, of course. But the Regent is more dangerous than his stats might suggest since he has command of the following sorceries, any one of which will take up a combat turn:

LEPROSY Requires throw of 8 or better on two dice. Causes opponent to begin to rot so that he loses 10% of his LIFE POINTS each combat turn following the casting of the spell.

BLIGHT Requires throw of 6 or better on two dice. Paralyses opponent completely for two combat rounds.

TIMETRAP Requires throw of 9 or better on two dice. Causes opponent to return to an earlier section of the adventure, determined as follows:
Two dice are thrown and the result multiplied by 10. Final total indicates relevant section number.

CRACK OF DOOM Requires throw of 8 or better. If successful, Regent will clap his hands and the resultant noise will remove 50 of his opponent's LIFE POINTS.

FIREBOLT Requires throw of 9 or better. Causes lightning to strike opponent for the loss of 75 LIFE POINTS.

Note: Each of the above spells will cost the Regent a double dice throw of LIFE POINTS if he elects to use them. This cost is payable whether or not the dice subsequently show the spell to be effective.

The Regent is also equipped with a magical sword for hand to hand encounters. It operates as a +10 sword in the first combat round, a +20 sword in the second combat round, and a +20 multiplied by the result of a single dice roll in every third combat round. If the combat lasts more than three rounds, the sword reverts to +10 on the fourth round and begins its cycle again.

Stephen Donaldson

The Chronicles of Thomas Covenant, the Unbeliever

'Comparable to Tolkien at his best . . . will certainly find a place on the small list of true classics.' *Washington Post*

'An irresistible epic.' *Chicago Daily News*

'The most original fantasy since *Lord of the Rings* and an outstanding novel to boot.' *Time Out*, London

'Intricate, absorbing, these volumes create a whole new world.' *Sunday Press*, Dublin

The First Chronicles of Thomas Covenant, the Unbeliever

LORD FOUL'S BANE £2.50
THE ILLEARTH WAR £2.50
THE POWER THAT PRESERVES £2.50

The Second Chronicles of Thomas Covenant

THE WOUNDED LAND £2.50
THE ONE TREE £1.95
WHITE GOLD WIELDER £2.50

FONTANA PAPERBACKS

Rules of Combat

First Strike

Roll two dice for your character; two for the enemy. Add to the result the SPEED, COURAGE, LUCK of each. Highest moves first.

To begin Combat, each takes turn.

Successful Hit

Roll two dice. Score of 7 or more indicates hit. But for every 10 full points of SKILL, take one point off hit requirements. For every 72 LUCK points, take one point off hit requirements.

Damage

Subtract modified strike score from actual number rolled and multiply by 10. Modify by STRENGTH: for every 8 points STRENGTH, add one to DAMAGE. Modified also by weapon, check Table on page 18.

Avoiding Death

If LIFE POINTS 0 or below, roll two dice, multiply by 8. If final score is less than LUCK, then start fight again.

Endurance

Length of battle depends on STAMINA. Divide figure by 10 for number of rounds.

Gaining Skill

For every fight you survive, add one to SKILL.